Praise for *Stained*

"Selina is an engaging central character, a focused and tenacious young woman who refuses to be broken by her traumatic experience and ultimately determines to shape her future herself. Through the compelling plot and carefully structured narrative, Khan gives voice to women whose stories are rarely heard and raises a series of complex and challenging cultural, social and moral questions."

— *Yorkshire Post*

"Khan's characterisation and dramatic plot speak for women who currently do not have a voice at all, and expose the traumatic abuse faced by women in many cultures."

—*South Asian Post*

"*Stained*, draws readers in with the effortless combination of an intense storyline that is tinged with elements of the unexpected. Khan's skillful characterization facilitates a relationship with the heroine, and allows the reader to become immersed in her world."

—*Asian Lite News*

"Khan has written a contemporary *Tess of the D'Urbervilles*, a heart-wrenching and engrossing tale that challenges the definition of morality through the story of a wronged young woman fighting to come to terms with harsh realities and finding empowerment along the way."

—*Booklist*, Caitlin Brown

"Stained examines the pressures of cultural taboos and sensitivities faced by women in society, and how they affect their life profoundly. Ultimately, it explores human endurance in the face of extreme adversity, and the extent to which, eventually, one is left with nothing but hope. The plot and characters draw the reader in from the very first page. Abda Khan has skilfully produced a novel that is both compelling and thought-provoking. A thoroughly captivating book."

—Julian Knight, Member of the British Parliament,
Author & former BBC Journalist

"Khan [has been praised] for her simple style, eloquence and honest storytelling. Her authenticity and down-to-earth approach to a compelling and emotional story are brave and refreshing."

—*Anokhi Media*

"Abda Khan is a fresh voice in British-Asian literature. Stained is fast-paced and enjoyable. Selina, the main character in Stained, is deep and impressive."

—*Raavi Magazine*

"There's a lot to be learned from such characters as Selina. More, though—her story was of finding herself DESPITE the path life set her on. The prose throughout was melodic and, though dark at points, maintained a poetic beauty I admire. Though this is first-person narrative from Selina's perspective, I feel Abda Khan painted the rest of the characters in ways that made them live and breathe from the pages...this book touched me deeply..."

—*Betwixt the Pages*

"Selina is a superb character—very easy to like and empathize with, and her voice feels completely natural and real. I also love the way Abda has woven in the various strands about culture and identity, and the cultural clash that takes place in the homes and hearts of South Asian families in Britain. The differing viewpoints of Selina and her mother come across very sharply, but with a warmth that's often lacking. I found the story to be dark and shocking in places, but this only added to my enjoyment of it. Stained showcases what, for me, is the often almost hopeless reality of life for so many girls, and the ending, although sad, is refreshingly honest and real. I think this is a much-needed antidote to the London media-friendly 'sari's and samosas' claptrap that often masquerades as authentic British South Asian fiction. I love that it's set in Bradford and Brum, and that Abda has left no stone unturned, especially in dealing with patriarchy and the predatory nature of some men. I thoroughly enjoyed it."

—Bali Rai, Celebrated British Author

"An inspiring and empowering story about a young British Muslim girl's determination for independence and self-regulation. Selina's story is captivating, with so many twists and turns that I read it in one sitting!"

—R Hanif

"It's a very well-written book, engaging and definitely recommendable. Riveting descriptions bring the story to life, especially in the most emotive passages...definitely a page turner that will keep you hooked. "

—*Eastern Eye Newspaper*

"Loaded with painful lessons from the contemporary immigrant experience"

—*The Weekly Voice*

"Lawyer and author Abda Khan will tell you she has no professional training as a writer, but real life experience proved more than enough preparation for her debut novel, Stained."

—*Anokhi Media*

Stained

Abda Khan

Harvard Square Editions
New York
2016

In memory of my beautiful Mum

Chapter 1: The Kite Must Fly!

RUN!

Run faster!

I could hear the words loud in my head as I scurried away. It was a beautiful, warm June evening, but my body was shivering.

I was sprinting like a maniac, although I had no idea how, as though some gust of mysterious wind was dragging me along, like a flimsy kite on a string; the kite flies high only because of the wind, but descends lifelessly to the ground without it.

I alone could hear the silent screams in my head as I raced across the park toward home. And only I could hear the tick tock, tick tock, tick tock. It was still ringing in my ears. Tick tock, tick tock, tick tock. Piercing through my head, in and out, around and around. Tick tock, tick tock, tick tock.

When I got to the front gate of our old, stone, terraced house, I stopped dead. They could not see me like this. I clung hard to the curls of iron at the top of the gate, the whites of my knuckles protruding, and dimming the redness of the scratches on my hands.

I wiped my tears with my sleeve, leant over and slowly opened the gate. I tentatively went up the two stone steps, and peered through the letterbox. Neither of them was in the hallway, so I entered the house, painstakingly quietly, and crept up the stairs. Just as I reached the landing, I heard my mum's voice shouting from the bottom of the stairs.

'Selina, you're back already? You're early today. Dinner is nearly ready, come down.' Her voice was loud and motherly. She was wholly oblivious to the difficulty that I was in. 'It's your favourite, chicken *haleem*, and I've just finished the *rotis* so they are piping hot.' As though that would make everything alright! A sob nearly escaped my lips.

I took another deep breath, which did nothing except make my head spin even more. I steadied myself on the banister, closed my eyes and shouted back, trying bravely to hide the quiver in my voice.

'No, *ammee*, I'm not hungry. I've got a headache, that's why I came back early. I'm going to go straight to bed; I'll come down and eat later on if I feel up to it.'

I didn't wait for her reply, but instead stumbled to my bedroom, locked the door, and with my back and long hair scraping all the way down against the door, I fell to the floor in a messy heap. I sobbed uncontrollably, but quietly, biting my hand hard. I could not help but cry, but was adamant that my mum and brother should not hear me. So, to accompany my copious, riotous tears were my deathly silent screams, stifled between my teeth and knuckles, with nowhere to go.

From the corner of my eye I noticed the deep red stain on my carpet. It made me jump; my eyeballs fixed upon it as though I had been hypnotized into staring at the bloody patch. The sight of it caused me to lapse into a quiet, heady panic, and I felt sick. I would have to wash it away, I thought, I would have to get it out. It had to go. It *must go*. In reality, however, it wouldn't matter how hard I scrubbed, and how much I willed it to vanish. It would prove to be indelible. Cleaning the carpet could wait, however, for I had to see to myself first. But I feared that these stains would not wash away either.

As I stood under the steaming shower, my tears continued to run. They rolled into the hot water and became one long entity. Like the sweet river and the salty sea when they meet. There is no partition. Where does the river end, and the sea begin? They just meet and become one. Like my salty tears and the hot water. I closed my eyes. I wanted to see nothing, I wanted to feel nothing. I just wanted darkness, blackness, but my eyes kept dragging me back to it all. And still, all I could hear was the tick tock, tick tock, tick tock. I put my hands over my ears, desperately trying to banish the incessant noise that was on repeat in my head, to no effect. How was I ever going to get that sound out of my head? Tick, tock, tick, tock, tick tock....

Chapter 2: I am Selina

HOW DID THIS EVEN happen to me? The dire situation in which I found myself astonished me. There was a time when life was simple, when all I dreamed of was getting into law school, and going on to fulfil my ambitions of practising as a leading human rights lawyer. Having been offered a place at my university of choice, I should have been ecstatic, but with everything that had happened, it just didn't feel as great as it should have.

I am Selina Hussain. People tell me I am a bright, beautiful eighteen-year-old young woman. But I think I am still a girl. I am not very sophisticated, or worldly-wise, or even streetwise, as some young women of my age are. I am a simple creature; straightforward, youthful, perhaps even naive.

Up to this point, I had so far come through life with not much to cause me great concern, bar the odd sibling fight or girlfriend disagreement. Life was pretty good, until everything fell apart. My change in fortunes for the worse started when I was over half way through my 'A' levels; the first of many unthinkable things happened to me. My world and life as I had known it since the day I was born changed forever. Last year, my father died in a car accident, leaving me and my family devastated.

He went before his time, being only fifty-nine years old, and his sudden death affected me profoundly. My older sister, Henna, now twenty-four, had married the year before dad died, and was living happily with her husband Faisal in Manchester. She had always been closer to our mum, Rashida, as was my little fourteen-year-old brother, Adam. I know I had been the apple of my dad's eye. We had been undeniably close. I had always fought my dad's corner in any matter that required it, and he had always done the same for me.

So the absence of my father left a monumental, empty hole in my life, which just could not be filled. And at first, it wouldn't sink in; I couldn't convince myself that he was actually gone. My protector, my friend, my champion, my unfailingly devoted, loyal father was gone! Who was I going to have a laugh with now? Who was I going to drag to the shops for the new mobile phone that I really needed? Who was going to cheer me up when things didn't go as I wanted?

In some crazy way, school was the thing, the place that kept me going. It had some sense of normality still. Home was not 'normal' anymore. It never could be with my father gone. I loved my mother, of course, and Adam, but with my father missing, how was I ever going to be happy in that house again? At least nothing had really changed at school. My teachers, my subjects, my friends, they all instilled a sense of reassurance and familiarity in me so that sometimes, just sometimes, I was able to forget the sadness. And there was Abigail Lucas, my best friend for the last seven years, for all the time we had been at upper school. Abigail was a good-humoured sort of a girl, always carrying a cheerful persona that few could match. She was often full of jolly banter. All that, along with her large, bright, blue eyes and big, wide smile added to her charm. We had a tightly knit friendship, and we were always there for each other whenever it mattered. Abigail leaned on me when her parents shattered her happy existence by divorcing very acrimoniously three years ago, and she was there for me when I lost my father.

After my dad died, everything changed. Life changed, and we, as a family, changed. Before becoming a widow, my mother had been such a jolly, carefree person, singing in the kitchen to her favourite *qawwalis* and Bollywood film songs whilst she cooked and did the housework. She was quite traditional at heart; she wore *salwar kameez* most of the time, with a matching scarf wrapped around her neck at home, but loosely around her head when she went out. She always had on her traditional gold bangles, and usually tied her long, dark hair in a bun or weaved it into a plait. Her love of all things traditional extended to her taste in music. She especially loved the Mohammed Rafi romantic numbers, not to mention her beloved Ustad Nusrat Fateh Ali Khan. I remembered how she used to belt out *"Dam Dam Ali Ali"* at the top of her voice, and when we as kids used to hear her singing along to this one, we knew she was in a good mood and we could ask her for anything. She was always the first one to laugh at a joke, or a comedy sketch on television. But that wasn't the case anymore. That all went after my dad's death; it all disappeared. Just like things disappear in a magician's puff of smoke. Gone. I understood my mum's pain and sadness. That I could cope with, but it was more than that. She fretted about every little thing. She always saw herself as just this Pakistani housewife, someone who had come over at the age of seventeen to be a wife. Although she did speak good English and was bright enough, she had never worked outside the house; dad had always been the sole breadwinner. She had looked after the home and the children, and until a few years ago, her parents-in-law as well, never worrying about the bills or anything else for that matter. She just wasn't like her old self anymore.

I will never forget the one time, before dad died, when I won a national poetry competition and was invited to the awards ceremony in London. We were given two first-class rail tickets to go down, so it was agreed that mum would come with me. When we entered the first class compartment, the snotty woman who worked on the train looked at us as though we were something she had dragged in with her shoe. She had big, googly blue eyes and thin, pursed lips. I could never forget her blonde beehive either. "Excuse me, you do know this carriage is for first-class passengers," she said, as she tapped my mum's shoulder when we were walking past. "Oh? Please the ticket look, me no speaking English, what say." I couldn't believe it! My mum spoke very good English. The googly-eyed woman gave a wry smile and looked at our tickets, but the smirk soon turned to a grimace and she begrudgingly handed them back, informing us we were in the right carriage. "You don't say?" said my mum to her, hand on hip, looking straight into her googly eyes, and commanding the attention of the whole carriage. "Now you listen to me lady. You do know that brown people are allowed to travel first-class as well white people? The days of the Raj are well and truly over, so put that in your pipe and smoke it!"

Wow! Go mum! These had been my thoughts at the time.

But now that my father was gone, my mother was like a shadow of her old self. More than anything else, she felt scared—of everything. Scared of any kind of paperwork, scared of how she was going to make ends meet as she was having to survive on her widow's pension and child benefits, scared of how she was going to get things around the house fixed. She was scared of responsibility in any shape or form. She had developed a nervous kind of seriousness that pervaded her entire character. And now she worried about her children, constantly. And in particular, she agonised about me.

A few months ago, I was at a low ebb, and decided to take up an offer from one of the boys in the sixth form to bunk off school and go into town. I would never normally have dreamed of doing this; I had never bunked off school before, and did have to think twice before agreeing to go with Andy. I was not in the least bit interested in Andy. He wasn't bad looking as it went, but he could be a bit dim, and that was always a turnoff, as far as I was concerned. But, I fancied a bit of an escape from all the pressure of school. He may have had other things in mind, in fact, he did as it turned out, but I was so down in the dumps that I saw the offer as a welcome distraction. I was in mourning for my dad still. Things were getting on top of me, and I hadn't done my Economics essay anyway, so I thought, why not, even though it wasn't like me. We made our way around to the back of the shopping mall for a bit of fresh air, and went and sat on a bench overlooking the little landscaped garden area, which was pretty much deserted, barring the odd passerby.

'So, hope you don't mind me asking, but what religion are you?' Andy asked me, as we both sipped from our cans of soft drinks.

'What's that got to do with the price of eggs?' I retorted, giving him a stern sideways look in the process. 'But if you must know, I'm Muslim. And before you start, we're not all terrorists.'

'I wasn't thinking that. Is that the religion where you're allowed to have four wives?' he asked excitedly, his smile widening, revealing a crooked bottom tooth, and his eyes dripping with thoughts that I didn't even want to conjecture about.

'Technically, yes, but in reality, it's a tough thing to achieve. You see, to take a second wife, you need the first one's permission. If she doesn't agree, and you'd never catch me or any other Muslim girl I know actually agreeing to it, then either you have to forget about your second one or divorce the first one to marry number two. If number one agrees, and you go on to have two wives, then you have to treat them absolutely equally. The both have to have the same sized house each, the same standard of living, you have to give them equal amounts of money for their living expenses, you have to buy them the same presents, spend the same amount of time with them, blah blah blah. So you see; it's actually not that easy to have more than one wife, and to have four, well that would be crazy. Not to mention that you'd have to be a millionaire.'

'So then why are Muslim men allowed four wives?' Andy asked, looking very puzzled. Explaining this was always difficult. Explaining it to Andy was going to be quite a challenge.

'Well, before Islam, men were allowed to have loads of wives, as in there was no limit, and it didn't matter how the men treated them. The four wife rule came in firstly as a restriction, but also because during the wars, a lot of the men were killed in battle, and so many women were widowed. There was a shortage of men, and so each man was allowed to take up to four wives if he wanted. But he had to be fair to all of them. And women were given a lot of rights as well, rights they didn't have before Islam. But as ever, you find that men always twist things to their own advantage and bend the rules as they want.' As I finished my sentence, I noticed Andy was staring at me very intensely with his piercing, blue eyes, leaning over slightly, reeking of far too much aftershave. He smelt like the tropical-scented bathroom cleaner at home.

'You're really pretty you are. I've been dying to get you on your own for ages. You're like some forbidden fruit or something. I make it so obvious that I think you're gorgeous, and I fancy you to bits, but I don't think you notice I even exist most of the time.'

Without further word or warning, he lunged right over and started to give me a big sloppy kiss. Unbeknown to me, one of the local gossips, Mrs Begum, who lived a few houses down from us, happened to be walking by and saw the grope and snog, and naturally went and spread it all about. What she hadn't seen, because she never bothered to hang around, was the bit where I had pushed Andy off as I hadn't enjoyed his kiss at all. I had found it slobbery and disgusting, and I ran straight to the ladies to wash my mouth out! Needless to say, I came back and told Andy in no uncertain terms where he stood with this forbidden fruit; it was a rare specimen that was for display only, labelled "do not touch". I had very much said this to Andy half angrily, but half in jest. However, I was soon going to learn that these words would resonate much more deeply.

Before long, word got back to my mum that I had been seen with a boy, and he was not any boy, but in fact I had a *gora* boyfriend, and we had been boyfriend and girlfriend for ages, and actually I'd had quite a few boyfriends and was such a mess about and a tease where the boys at school were concerned. I wouldn't have minded, but I knew for a fact that Mrs Begum's daughter really was the local tart! Whereas I didn't wear a headscarf, she used to leave the house with her *hijab* on, and when she got to school, she used to run straight to the toilets, fling off her headscarf, paste on the make-up and head out with her boyfriend, or rather one of her boyfriends, as she was known to have more than one on the go. Nothing had changed much now that she was at the college. What hypocrites.

My mum was furious with me, and explained how respectable Pakistani girls did not have boyfriends, and how could I allow such talk to bring shame upon her in this way, and what will people say, and if I get myself a reputation, then no one will want to marry me, I will be dependent on my future sister-in-law, and I will die a lonely old maid with no children of my own to look after me. She spent the best part of an hour relentlessly chiding me, and then I spent the next hour reassuring her that Andy was not my boyfriend, and that I didn't have a boyfriend full stop. It was hard to know at the end of it all if my mum believed me or not, but needless to say she wasn't best pleased, and told me in a nutshell, that I should not behave in such a way so as to bring the family name and honour into disrepute. This episode with Andy, and my mum's general tension, culminated in an important announcement she made concerning my future.

She was in the kitchen busy chopping the onions for the curry she was about to start cooking. It was *achari* chicken today. She didn't have to say anything, I could tell by the aroma of the spice blend that she had roasted and ground; seeds of fennel, cumin, coriander, nigella and fenugreek. The fragrance was unmistakable; mouth wateringly enticing. I had made the *chappati* dough for her earlier on, as it was the one chore my mum really disliked. I had a quick nosey over her shoulder, and then decided to make myself some coffee. As I flicked the kettle on, my mum left what she was doing, washed and dried her hands and went and sat at the dining table.

'Come Selina, I must talk with you about something very important.' She beckoned to me to come and join her. 'I didn't know exactly when to tell you, but now I think the time is right.'

I finished making my coffee, stirring the spoon carefully around in my bear-shaped mug. I came and sat opposite her, and speculated in my own mind as to what it might be that my mother was in such a hurry to talk to me about. Really, I hadn't the foggiest.

'Well, you know how I worry about you, and it is my one wish now to see you married and settled, just like your sister. Henna is thankfully very happy with her husband. I would not have thought about this so early on had it not been for the sadness in our lives of your father leaving us so suddenly. And there is also the fact that you have been messing around with boys at school, and a white boy at that. But in truth, your father's death changes everything. In our culture, unmarried children, especially daughters, are a burden on their parents. I don't really mean a physical or financial burden, more like emotional. And making sure you are married off is my duty alone now. Well, coming to the point, you know that your uncle Ali in Birmingham has been very keen on your marrying his son, mainly because the son himself is so crazy about you. We have been talking about it for some time now.'

I was aware that about a year ago, there had been some talk of a possibility of the union, but I had no idea about any recent discussions. Anyway, as far as I could remember, my

father had said that they would think about it only after I had
finished my degree, and even then it would be subject to me
being agreeable to the marriage proposal. I was aware that
Uncle Ali's son, Sohail, fancied me. It was obvious, but in all
honesty, I had no feelings for him.

'As you have been offered a place at Birmingham University
to study Law,' continued my mum, 'and your wish is to go
there over and above any of the other universities you have
applied for, I have decided that you shall marry Sohail straight
after your exams, move down and settle in there, and then I
will not have to worry about you studying away from home, as
you will be with your husband.'

'What?' I shrieked, banging my beloved bear mug down on
the table, surprised that I hadn't broken it with the sudden
force I inflicted upon it. But I was seeing red. 'How could you
decide such a thing without asking me first? Don't I even get a
say? Mum, I can't agree to this—firstly, I'm way too young to
be getting married, and secondly, I don't even like him. I can't
marry someone I barely say two words to whenever we meet! I
can't believe you agreed to it! You'll to have to call it off!'

My mum looked straight at me with her most piercing
stare, designed to inform me, without actually saying it, that I
was now beginning to overstep the mark and should think
about winding my neck in.

'I will do no such thing. What is this *bakwas*, this rubbish
you are talking? Have you lost all hold of your senses? *Paghal!*
Where else are you going to find such a good *rishta*? Such a
great offer of marriage does not come along every day young
lady. I know you are a bit younger than your sister was when
she got married, and a few years younger than Sohail, but so
what? He is such a good catch. He is fine-looking, extremely
polite, and good-natured, and above all from what I have seen,
he thinks the world of you. That counts for a lot. They are
family, and that is why his parents are agreeable. Were they not

related to us, you would have no chance of securing such a wonderful betrothal.'

'Mum, listen to me,' I said, with a degree more respect in the tone of my voice this time, trying to break her flow, but my mum just carried right on.

'We are not of the same social status as them. We don't have very much; in fact, we have nothing apart from this small house and a few pounds in the bank. But they are a very wealthy family. They have a huge business, many properties, lots of money in the bank. They live in the most wonderfully upmarket area and in such magnificent houses. And they have a mansion in Islamabad, did you know that? Sohail is an accountant in the family business, and being the only son, he will inherit most, if not all of it anyway: the business, the properties, the lot. And you know he has his own house, so you won't even have to live with in-laws. And he loves you. I mean, you are getting the total package, how often does that happen for a girl? What is wrong with you? You will be living in the lap of luxury. You will never ever want for anything. To decline such a kind-hearted, generous offer would be disrespectful and disgraceful. What *izzat* would I have left in the wider family? Anyway, I have given my word now so it is final. No more discussions, no more arguments!'

'But mum, dad said....'

'But mum nothing. I have said, so I have said, that's it. It is time for you to grow up young lady. Henna never gave me any of this lip. Your father spoilt you; that's the real problem here. But he's not here anymore, I am, and I have to do what I think is right. And you will go through with this wedding, you will not act dishonourably in any way so as to damage this family's reputation and standing within the *bradri* and community, and you will keep our *izzat* intact. An opportunity like this will not come again, and I won't allow you to pass it by. That's it, *bas*. Enough.'

Chapter 3: The Battle with Economics

'YOU CAN'T MARRY HIM!' Abigail said. She was predictably horrified when I recalled the gist of the conversation between me and my mother, on Monday back at school.

I finished the last bit of my tuna and cucumber sandwich as we sat and chatted during our late lunch break in a quiet corner of the sixth form common room.

'You're telling me! There's no way I can even think of marrying him, or anyone else, before I finish my studies and start my career. I don't even fancy him. I know he's got a thing for me, but I'm just not fussed about him; having said that, I can't talk to my mum about it just yet. She'll give me merry hell. I've gotten so behind with my work and I'm really feeling the pressure. I need to just knuckle down and catch up. I don't want to mess up my exams. Before my dad died, I was a straight-A student, and I know I can be again. I'm going to wait until the exams are over and then tell her. It's only a matter of weeks now.'

'But she will have arranged everything by then,' Abigail said, whilst tightening her long, unruly ponytail, her bright eyes widening as she spoke. 'Don't you think it might be a bit late, especially if she's talking about having the wedding in the middle of July! I've never seen this guy your mum wants to hook you up with, but you are gorgeous Selina. You can have any guy you want. I would give anything to have a figure like yours, not to mention your silky, long hair and perfect skin!' The more she spoke, the more dramatic she sounded, and behaved, as she grabbed a strand of my hair and flicked it back in jest.

'Well, I don't think she is planning a big wedding on our end, because to be honest, we can't really afford it. She's thinking of just arranging the *nikah* ceremony at the mosque and feeding everyone there. The mosque people were really good to us when dad died, and I'm sure they will look after us again. They won't charge us for cancelling. It's Sohail's family who will be orchestrating the grand, Bollywood-style wedding; I'm sure they would want professional musicians, *bhangra* dancers, half a dozen fancy cars, of course, the obligatory ice sculpture, and probably a twelve-tier wedding cake. Well, you get the gist. And truthfully, I don't care about them. I've never liked them, and to this day they've never asked me once what I think, or if I'm okay with it all. I'm sure they think I should be grateful to them that they are allowing me to marry their precious son! They all came up yesterday, the whole lot of them, with all their pretentious ideas about the wedding outfits and jewellery. Honestly, they're such snooty poops. I just had to sit there and smile through it all. And they took my measurements for some ludicrously gory Swarovski crystal-studded, fairy-tale wedding dress. From the way they described the dress, it's going to be so shiny and sparkly, I would probably get mistaken for a Christmas tree. Honestly, the barefaced cheek of it. Well, they can spend as much money as they want; they can buy as much bling as they can afford; I'm not going through with it. They think they're so much better than us. Just because we're not well off and they're filthy rich, they presume I couldn't possibly say no. But I can't go through with it. It's not what I want. I will just have to find a way out.'

As she listened to me intently, Abigail's face clouded over, and she let out a muffled sigh, as if to say that she didn't quite believe my assurances that I had the situation under control.

'I hope so, but I'm worried about you. What if you can't say no? What if the pressure becomes too much? You do remember I'm going away with mum the day after my last exam to stay with my grandparents in Spain, and won't be back until August? So I won't even be here to help you through the whole ordeal.'

'I know; I wish you were going to be here, but don't worry, by the time you get back it will all be done and dusted. Right then, time to go see Miss Baker about my Economics. I hate this subject. I'm doing fine with History and English lit, but I need A's in all of my subjects if I'm going to do law. Here goes.'

When I walked into her room, Miss Baker was wearing a solemn look on her face. She had her half-moon glasses on the end of her nose, as she sat at her desk examining some sheets of paper.

'Now then, Selina,' she began, in her very official-sounding tone, as I sat in the chair opposite her on the other side of her desk. 'We really must talk about your Economics. I appreciate what a difficult year it has been for you, but I am very concerned that you are struggling to such an extent that you may not be able to turn things around in time for the exams. Your last test result was quite a bit off target. Is there anything I, or any other member of staff, can do to help? I see that you are on target with your other two 'A' levels, so it's just this subject.'

It *was* just this subject, and I couldn't very well tell her that the teaching for this subject was hideous compared to my other two. Miss Baker meant well, but she couldn't teach Economics to save her life. She was as well-versed with the intricacies of Economics as I was with zoo keeping. I knew that I just had to knuckle down and go through everything myself. The basic revision guides would be more useful than this shower ever could be.

'I think maybe I need to start going back over the material with a fine-tooth comb Miss, and make sure I go over any homework or essays that I have missed, or not done very well in. And do lots of past papers perhaps? I think I will be fine, but if I do need any extra help, I will let you know.' Miss Baker seemed satisfied enough with my proposal, even though I knew that nothing had changed, and I was going to go on finding this subject tough. But we left it at that.

The topic of my battle with Economics continued that evening, although the discussion did not involve my fourteen-year-old brother, as Adam had his head down, and was lost in his own world playing some game on his phone. He had shot up in height recently, and was going through a slightly spotty phase, as well as behaving like a typical, teenage boy who conversed in speech that rarely comprised more than half a sentence.

I desperately wanted to do well in my exams and get to university. I didn't want to end up like an old housewife before my time, hoovering the carpets and washing the dishes all day long. I had goals that I wanted to achieve. Mum and I happened to be talking about Economic when at that precise time Zubair and Sajda Qureshi turned up.

'We were just passing, so we thought we would look in and see how you are all doing,' Zubair said as they both entered the house.

'So lovely to see you. Please, come on in,' said mum, who greeted them as warmly as she possibly could, and then showed them into the living room, where she quickly sorted the scatter cushions on the sofa before they sat down. She had a lot of time for the Qureshis. Sajda was a tutor at college, working a few days a week, and a couple of evenings, teaching English to students from overseas. And she often called round to see how my mum was doing, more so since dad had died. She had a kind, pretty face, and had wavy dark, brown, shoulder-length hair, although she often told me that her hair used to be as black and long—to the hips—as mine when she was my age. She was a genuinely caring sort of a lady.

Zubair Qureshi was probably one of the most respected men in the local community. He was now most likely in his late forties, and still quite a handsome man. But more importantly, at any rate to my mum and everyone else of her generation and older, he was a highly educated and pious man, being a Senior Lecturer in Business Studies at the University, and also a member of the Mosque committee. He had helped my mum hugely on the occasion of the death of my dad, arranging the funeral prayers, the funeral car, the burial, the food at the mosque for the mourners. He had been more than generous with his time and efforts, not to mention making things financially easier for our family through his post at the mosque. He was well known by all for his benevolence in serving the community, as well as for helping a number of charities, volunteering regularly both here and on overseas trips. If anyone in the local community needed help of any kind, he was usually the first person they turned to, and he never said no. And our two families went back a long way. It was true to say that my mum couldn't have got through that time when my dad died, and the aftermath, without the help uncle Zubair had given her, and for that she would be eternally grateful. She genuinely looked upon him like a younger brother.

Their two sons were away from home studying at their respective universities, so Zubair and Sajda naturally had more time on their hands. They found it easier to drop by for visits, and to help with community events. And Zubair had more time to devote to those who needed his assistance.

'So, how are your studies going?' asked Sajda, turning toward Adam, and then toward me as I walked in with a tray of tea and the best biscuits. I was always sure to follow my mum's strict instructions for these two guests, to bring in a plate of the finest biscuits selected from the posh, chocolate biscuit tin, and to serve the tea from our best tea set, of course.

'I'm fine, Aunty, I'm just happy that I haven't got proper exams like Selina. She's well stressed,' replied Adam, momentarily lifting his head from the game he was playing on his mobile phone. At least he had spoken with a bit of clarity, which was rare, as he mumbled most of the time.

'Actually, Selina is having trouble with her Economics,' said my mum, answering for me. 'She is absolutely great with her other subjects, but Economics is giving her a lot of trouble.'

'Well, I can help her if you like,' Zubair said as he reached for a chocolate finger. 'I did my degree in Business with Economics, and obviously a large part of what I teach involves Economics in one way or another. If you want, I can give her some lessons.'

'That would be amazing!' my mum said with a big smile on her face. 'And I can pay you—'

'Nonsense! I won't hear of it. That is the most ridiculous thing you have ever said to me *baji*. Me, take money off someone who is like an older sister to me? Not a chance. So, Selina, how long until your Economics exams?'

'Just under four weeks, and there's only a day's gap between the two papers,' I replied.

'Well, if you come over in the evenings, perhaps twice a week, say for two hours each time, I think that will be sufficient to go through the material. I think once you understand the basic concepts, the rest will follow easily enough. Bring all your books and notes with you. Is that alright with you dear?' he asked, turning to his wife.

'That is absolutely fine. No problem at all. In fact, Zubair is pretty good at this, and not just because he lectures. He's helped the kids in the family too. He's always helped the boys, obviously, and years ago, he helped my sister Raheela with her exam revision. Goodness, that was a long time ago, wasn't it Zubair?'

'Oh, yes about fifteen, maybe sixteen years ago,' he replied.

'Shall we say, Tuesdays and Thursdays, around seven o'clock?' Sajda asked whilst placing her teacup back down after the last sip. 'I'm not usually working on those evenings so I can provide the refreshments.'

'Yes, thanks, that's really kind of you.' I said.

So that was sorted. And to be truthful, I was relieved that now I might just have a chance of pulling that grade up to get me on to my Law degree.

Chapter 4: Tick tock, tick tock

I GOT READY for my first lesson with mixed feelings. Zubair was like an uncle, and I wasn't sure about being taught by an uncle-like figure. It was going to be hard for me to switch to seeing him as a teacher. But I had always observed him as a calm and good-hearted man, and I really did need the help. It seemed from what his wife said that he was pretty good at it. He did teach for a living after all.

I went into the kitchen and found my mum putting the shopping away. I had a quick glass of orange juice and gobbled a banana, which invited a telling off from my mum.

'Don't eat so fast,' she said, 'or you will end up with a tummy ache, and I don't have any *ajwain* seeds in at the moment, although I do have *saunf.*'

Ajwain seeds, or bishops weed as they were known in English, were the only bad-tummy remedy in our house; tried and trusted by generation upon generation of Pakistani housewives from one village to the next up and down the length and breadth of our native land, and this revered remedy was available in probably every Pakistani household within these shores too. In its absence, fennel seeds were the next best thing, boiled up into a tea. I assured her that my tummy was fine, promptly kissed her goodbye on her cheek, and began the walk from our house to theirs.

We lived in an inner-city area of Bradford that was very much multi-cultural, and the majority of the householders now were of sub-continental Asian origin. There were still a few indigenous white families, some who had lived here for years, but most had moved away into suburban areas, and their properties had been taken over by second and third generation

immigrants, as well as a good sprinkling of recent Polish and
other Eastern European settlers. My mum knew virtually
everyone who lived on our street, and there was a strong
community atmosphere.

Our little house was in the middle of a long street that was
full of identical little terraced houses, in an area full of lots of
streets that looked exactly the same; row after row after row,
separated by the gullies which ran between each line of the old,
stone properties. Most of them didn't have a front garden to
speak of, and just a small yard at the back. Some of the houses
still had the old coal sheds at the bottom of the yard, but of
course, they were no longer used for coal, more for storage of
bikes, tools and other bits and pieces. Others had taken the
coal sheds out to square off the yards, to pave them, or fill
them completely with tarmac, so they could park their cars.
The passages that ran between the streets at the back of the
houses were just about wide enough for the cars to gain access.
We didn't have a car anymore. But my mum put our yard to
good use. She grew her own rusty-red, deep-orange, and
mellow-yellow marigolds in any pots she could lay her hands
on—pretty pots, old buckets, even old, large, plastic tubs. And
she cultivated a small vegetable plot to one side where she
mainly grew her favourite herbs—mint, coriander and
fenugreek. But she also managed a good amount of spinach
and some spring onions. When she used these homegrown
goodies—the fresh curly coriander and the clover-shaped
fenugreek leaves, the chopped spring onions and spinach—in
her *pakora* batter, this resulted in her producing the world's
most flavoursome, soft yet crunchy melt-in-the-mouth *pakoras*
ever! We all told her that nobody made better *pakoras* than her,
although she was adamant that the *pakora wala* who used to
come round to their village in Pakistan with his wooden cart
laden with his hand-made snacks actually made the best
pakoras. And she said his *channa chaat* and *dahi bhalay* were to-
die-for. She said as soon as she used to hear the faintest sound

coming from away in the distance, she used to run up to the rooftop terrace, jumping several times to avoid stepping in the sprawling sea of red chillies drying in the sun, to look over into the distance to make sure it was actually the *pakora wala* that was coming toward their house. He would look like a dot weaving through the *kikar* trees and across the stream in the approach to the village. The voice would start becoming more distinct as he shouted his invitation to the villagers to come and purchase his goods. She said she knew it would not be long before he was pushing his cart by their house, and she would run, skipping over the drying chillies once again, to her mum or dad for some rupees. When we were younger, she used to imitate his voice—*"pakoray lay lo!"* A bit like the fruit stall sellers over here shouting, "Come and get your apples!" She would yell it in a long, drawn-out way, with a deep voice, as she would bring the hot *pakoras* with her homemade mint chutney from the kitchen. It was like a miniature piece of theatre. She didn't do it anymore.

The Qureshis house was about a ten-minute walk away, and in contrast to our old, terraced home with the backyard *cum* flower and vegetable plot, it was a detached property with pristinely manicured lawns in the front and back, in a development of new properties built around ten years ago, on the other side of the local park. This was considered to be the 'posh' area. Their large, modern house was what those who lived in the terraced houses like ours aspired to. It was what parents worked hard for, paying for extra private maths and science lessons for their children, hoping their sons would be doctors or lawyers and would be able to afford to help move their families up in the world. This would be the fruit of the parents' lifetime labour. But parents were becoming increasingly disappointed in this modern era. In days gone by, say when my dad got married, the sons would never dream of doing anything other than staying with their parents in an extended family setup. Nowadays, this was becoming less so; it was increasingly the trend that the sons were no longer living with their parents. What was previously regarded as merely a hideous, improbable thought was now a commonly occurring reality—the parents were living all alone, as having given their daughters away in matrimony, the sons, married or otherwise were nowhere to be seen; there was no one, single factor for this new, western inspired phenomenon. Some men who had taken brides from "back home" were still a part of their parents' household, as these wives were on the whole well versed in the concept of pleasing their husbands and in-laws for the opportunity given to them to come to this country and have a better life. They were domesticated and obedient, and these traditional values were ingrained into them. It was almost part of their DNA. In contrast, the girls born and bred in the UK were very different. These young women, were now becoming increasingly non-conformist, often possessing an almost rebellious independence, which meant the inevitable mother-in-law/daughter-in-law struggle. The traditional mum was a fool if she thought she could outwit this new breed of quick thinking, fiercely independently-minded Brit Pak girl. The mother would more often than not win the struggle for domestic dominance, but she would lose her son in the process. So, the son and wife would move out. Then there was a small but slowly growing scattering of the highly successful men who were absent because they had succeeded in their careers beyond anyone's wildest expectations. Even from quite a downtrodden community like ours, there were some young men, and indeed young women, who had reached the dizzy heights of noteworthy accomplishments in their fields—a high flying city stockbroker, an accountant who worked in New York, solicitors, barristers, doctors, research scientists, Google employees, Silicon Valley nerds, although sadly no Nobel Peace or Man Booker Prize winners—yet. All of these smart, prosperous young men and women were conspicuous by their absence, but at least the parents could boast about their achievements when they sat in a *mehfil* or gathering where such conversation inevitably arose. And for these parents, the ability to talk proudly about the extraordinary success of their children was some compensation for the emptiness they left behind. However, there were sons who were absent for the reasons their parents would sooner try and forget. Many were lost to drugs, pimping, and the general underbelly of crime. This vortex of the dark, turbulent world in which they existed had implications, which went far beyond affecting their own sorry lives. Take Aunty Fatima; not actually my aunty, but we call everyone Aunty and Uncle out of respect. She lives a few doors down from us. She has four daughters and one son. After the fourth girl—and even though she was expecting again—her husband left her; he moved away and remarried so he could try and go for the son which she couldn't give him. As fate had it, it turned out that she had a boy after all, although her husband never came back. She doted on that little boy, and in the end spoilt him rotten. When he grew up, he was wayward and rebellious, turned to drugs and general crime right across the board. He would disappear for weeks, even months, and when the money ran out, he would be back, and if need be he would beat his mum and the one sister that remained at home until he got what he wanted. The one time he battered his sister because she refused to hand over her gold jewellery that her mother had scrimped and saved to pay for in readiness for her upcoming nuptials. He beat her so badly she was hospitalised for a week. But nowadays they had some respite. In his general crime ridden existence, the son had gotten into a brawl and nearly killed a fellow druggy. He was sent to prison for ten years for attempted murder. Nothing to celebrate, but at least they could sleep at night without fear of him turning up to terrorise them.

* * *

Sajda opened the door to see I had arrived promptly. She showed me through their wide, airy hallway to the dining room at the front of the house, where the study session was to take place. The room was large and well-proportioned, and had a feel of grandeur about it, or at least that's the look the owners had tried to achieve. The large oval dining table, crafted from solid, dark wood, and the matching high-backed chairs, were very ornately designed. There was a grand, matching display cabinet at the side. It was sectioned with glass shelves in the top half. It housed a host of family photos in gleaming gold and silver-edged frames, and there were various expensive-looking show pieces made of fine crystal, marble and china.

'What would you like to drink Selina? Tea, coffee? Perhaps something to eat?' Sajda asked with a smile.

'Oh, no, it's very kind of you to ask Aunty, but I'm fine thanks, I had a snack and a drink before I came out,' I replied politely.

'*Assalam-u-alyakum*, Selina.' Uncle Zubair greeted me with the traditional Islamic hello as he walked in. He had a slight stubble, and his hair was casually flicked back. His face had very distinct, chiselled features; a slim nose, slightly narrow eyes, and for a man, he possessed very well defined temples and cheekbones. He was wearing casual clothes; black joggers and a light blue polo shirt. I rarely, if ever, saw him dressed like this. I was so used to seeing him in either a well-groomed, dark suit, which he wore to work, or his mosque attire of usually a white or grey *kurta* or *jubba*.

'*Walay kum asalam*,' I replied likewise.

He sat at the head of the table, and signalled for me to sit on the side, to his right, so I took out my books and pens, hung my bag and coat on the back of the chair, and we began.

The first lesson went really well. It was all very official, very much like being at school, but better. We went through the early part of the syllabus, and it was amazing how much more I understood it after he had explained things a couple of times over, but in a way that was easy to get, unlike my teachers at school who always seemed to communicate everything in the most long-winded and elaborate way possible. Aunty Sajda came in with tea and shortbread fingers around half way through, but other than that there were no distractions, and it was just, head down and get through as much as possible.

The next couple of lessons followed in the same vein. It took me a while to really get the nitty-gritty of managing the national economy, and to fully understand the contrasts between the different policies—supply side, monetary, exchange rate—but at the end of the third lesson, I felt like I was really getting there. These lessons were proving invaluable, and whilst I still had to make sure I revised well and remembered it all, I really thought that for the first time in nearly two years I actually got Economics. I was never going to be Chancellor of the Exchequer, but I was confident that at least now I did understand the basics.

The fourth session had come around soon enough, and I took my usual walk to their house across the park on this particularly warm evening. The park always looked sublime on warm summer days, and this late afternoon in June was no exception. The lake was glistening away in the distance; as though tiny, pearly bubbles of light were floating on its surface. It brought to mind the most unforgettable sight on our visit to Pakistan when I was younger. We children would run up to the rooftop terrace every evening as soon as dusk began to settle in, and watch the most spectacular light display ever, for down the hill, close by to the stream, we would see dozens, maybe hundreds of lights travelling in the air, going on and off. We discovered they were fireflies that actually had a light in their bottom! Or perhaps it was in their tummy. One of our older cousins trapped one in a glass jar for us, so we could have a proper look. He got into awful trouble from his mum, however, when he accidently dropped the jar and it smashed to smithereens, for she had been saving the jar especially so she could make a start on the lime pickle. The large lime tree that stood proudly in corner of the courtyard was full of fruit. These lights in the fireflies would glow intermittently and we would just gawp in amazement; it was like a glittering light show every evening. The lake in the park didn't have quite the same disco feel about it, but it certainly sparkled today.

The park looked like a picture postcard. The green of the grass contrasted with the blue of the lake, both alive and receptive to the gentle caress of the sun's rays. The silver birch, oak, and beech trees all stood majestically, basking in the warmth of the evening sun, and there was the unmistakable fragrance of quintessentially English summer flowers wafting about in the air; roses, jasmine and lily of the valley, all floated about atmospherically, coming at me from all directions.

I remembered how as kids, if the wind was right, our grandad used to bring us to the park and teach us to fly kites. Sometimes, my grandma used to tag along as well. I recall her telling me that in years gone by, when Eid was celebrated in Pakistan, after the men had returned from their Eid prayers at the mosque and the whole family had eaten the Eid feast of fragrant mutton *pilau* rice, spicy *keema koftas,* hot tandoori rotis and sweet cardamom vermicelli, everyone used to gather on their rooftops to fly their multi coloured kites. It was a fiercely fought, cross-generational competition, a matter of pride and honour. And it even provided the backdrop for many romantic interludes, when young men and young ladies were so busy exchanging glances that they would get their kites entangled with each others'. But, she had said with some sadness that such pleasures were now a thing of the past, even in Pakistan. People were now too busy playing with their mobile phones instead of with kites, and there were barely any kite makers to be found at the bazaars. I missed my grandparents, and all the good times we shared, and happily revisited the memories in my mind's eye as I strolled along.

We were scheduled to work on the topic of the international economy today. I thought about how far I had come with the subject. Zubair was a great teacher. If only the teachers at school were half as good as he was, I pondered, as I trundled along my usual path. If only I had got help sooner. But I was here now, and I really was very grateful. He was extremely patient, and had already made such a difference to my understanding of the subject.

I was in full swing with my other exams now, but luckily for me, it just so happened that the Economics papers were my last two exams, and with two weeks to go, hopefully I had enough time to cram everything in.

I went up to the door and rang the bell as usual, only this time I was surprised to see that it was Zubair who came to the door, not Sajda.

'*Assalam-u-alaykum* uncle.'

'*Walay kum asalam*,' he replied as he let me in.

He walked straight past the dining room and he showed me to the living room today, which was at the back of the house. I did think that was odd, as we always worked at the dining table, but he explained that one of the legs on the dining table was wobbly and needed fixing, so we had to make do with the living room. I went and sat on their luxury, chocolate-brown, leather sofa, took off my jacket and placed it on the armrest. I was careful not to knock over the china vase next to me. The elegantly arranged bouquet of flowers had been placed in the middle of the square, glass-topped side table.

'Where's aunty Sajda?' I asked, as I started taking my books out, and after I had piled them onto the matching glass topped coffee table in front of me, I looked up toward Zubair as he hadn't answered my question yet. I then repeated it in case he hadn't heard me the first time.

'Sajda had to do an evening class at college today. One of her colleagues is ill, so she had to step in,' he replied finally, his eyes fixed on me.

Something felt different, I thought to myself. I sensed that there was an odd atmosphere. Nothing that I could put my finger on, but something seemed strange nevertheless, maybe it was because aunty Sajda wasn't here. And the house was quieter than usual. Yes, that must be it, I concluded.

'Right then, shall we make a start,' he said, and came and sat on the sofa next to me. He sat very close to me. I felt decidedly uncomfortable, and so I moved over a little.

'So, here are the notes you asked me to bring,' I said, trying to hand them to him, but he didn't look down at the papers, as his eyes were still glued on my face. I placed them on to the coffee table.

'How was school today?' he asked.

'Well, I'm not really at school anymore; I just go in for the exams. I've been on study leave for a while now.'

He leaned back, and for a few seconds he didn't say anything.

'You know, I heard some talk a while back about you having a boyfriend. Is it true?' he asked.

I was shocked by his intrusive question. He had never talked to me about personal stuff before. We only ever discussed the work, nothing else, not ever. He was definitely not himself today.

'No, that was just a misunderstanding.'

'Really?'

'Of course I don't have a boyfriend, and I don't intend on having one. I'm serious about my studies, Uncle, and I really want to study law. My ambition is to become a human rights lawyer. I want to be able to fight for the underdog; just think of all the people in the world who are the victims of gross injustices. Having a boyfriend is not really part of the plan; it's not something that would be appropriate. I can assure you, Uncle, that I do understand that it wouldn't be right for me to go down that path.' Although I was taken aback by his question, I convinced myself that he was asking me as a concerned uncle, sort of like a father figure who, having heard the highly exaggerated gossip, was worried that I might be going off the rails or something.

'Oh, I see,' he said, raising his eyebrows slightly. 'It's just something I heard through the grapevine, that's all. You know how people like to talk. But then again, it wouldn't surprise me if you have lots of boys chasing you. You must get a lot of male attention.'

This line of conversation just didn't seem right now, and I was beginning to feel more than awkward. I wished he would stop with the superfluous chatter and get on with the lesson.

'No more than any other girl my age, I should think. Anyway, I don't really pay all that much attention to things like that. I don't have the time or the inclination to bother. Like I said, I'm focusing on my studies. It's what I want to do, and it's what my dad would have wanted. Even though he's not here anymore, I want to make him proud, and have the satisfaction of knowing in my heart that he would have been proud of me if he were still alive.'

I was hoping to be the first child in our family to get to university. My dad had not been a very educated man. He had been intelligent and capable enough, but he'd had to leave school at sixteen to support the family. He had worked hard in warehouses and in a chocolate factory in Leeds for the larger part of his working life. When I had been younger, this was great, and all three of us kids were never short of friends because of the constant supply of the milky, sweet bars, bags and boxes of chocolate that continued to flow our way in a steady stream. But now, none of us was at all fussed about anything remotely chocolaty.

'Of course, that goes without saying,' Zubair said, his voice prompting me to stop drifting away with my reflections about my father, and look toward him. He had a misty look in his eyes, and was now beginning to creep me out a little. 'Please, don't take any offence at my last comment. What I was trying to say, in my own peculiar way, is that whether you fully realise it or not, you are a very beautiful young lady Selina. You have the most decadently silky, long dark hair, and your eyes in their shape and colour are like two perfect almonds. Your lips encompass a sumptuous symmetry I have not seen in any other woman, and your skin is as though it were painted on; flawless, smooth, like milk and honey. Yes, you are indeed a thing of beauty; like this rose, see.'

He suddenly leaned over me and pulled out a single crimson rose from the bunch of flowers in the vase that was next to me. He slowly carried it across to himself, momentarily pausing with it in front of my face, the droplets of water falling onto my trousers, before bringing it in front of his own face, where he stared at it.

'Look how enchantingly beautiful this rose is, and so perfectly formed,' he said, stroking the rose up and down with his fingers. 'Just like you.' He turned his gaze toward me as he said those last three words.

'And just look at the petals,' he said, and he started pulling one off, slowly. He held it in his palm and then dropped it in front of me. And then another, and then another yet again, until there were at least half a dozen, deep red petals sitting in my lap. I was now beginning to feel a sense of panic creeping up inside of me, and my instinct told me to get the hell out of there. I didn't know what on earth was the matter with him today, but I figured I should just leave. Whilst trying my best to keep a cool exterior, I slowly got up from the sofa.

'I think maybe we should give the lesson a miss today Uncle.' I said as I got up.

He shot up and grabbed my wrist.

'Less of the uncle, my darling; call me Zubair, just Zubair. Come now, we haven't even got started yet, where are you going?' He was hurting my arm as he pulled me toward him.

Now I was in full-on panic mode.

Now I knew I just had to run.

Run, Selina, run!

'I'm not feeling very well; I want to go home. Please let go of me, you're hurting me. I want to go!' I said whilst trying to wriggle my wrist free.

He pushed me back onto the sofa, and to my shock, he leaned down and tried to kiss me.

'What are you doing? Let me go!' There was clear terror in my voice now, as I rapidly moved my head from one side to the other, trying to avoid his hungry mouth. I tried to escape, but he pushed me even harder onto my back, and I continued to writhe.

'I can't do that. I can't let you go home. You are simply intoxicating, mesmerising. I cannot let you go without showing you first how I feel. You must let me show you how I feel.'

'Let go of me. Please. Please!' I screamed.

But it was no use.

I was struggling in vain.

He felt heavy on top of me, pressing upon me like a solid metal weight holding down the thinnest sheet of paper. My screams and sobs were muffled by his might. I was no match for his brute force and unforgiving strength. I could yell no more. Never mind yell, I could barely breathe, and I lay there silently gasping and panting. I was withering away with no fight in me. And through it all I could smell him on me, all over me. He smelt musky, woody, sweaty. And vile. I was being mangled and compressed, bit-by-bit, inch-by-inch, limb by limb. Trampled on and violated for what seemed like an eternity. I could hear the pendulum of the large, walnut clock hanging on the wall as it swung from side to side. Tick tock. Tick tock. Tick tock. I could swear it was getting louder. When would it all stop? Tick tock, tick tock, tick tock. I could feel the trickle of my warm tears, rolling down and collecting in my ears, until they were full, and when my ears could hold no more, they flowed down my neck. I closed my eyes. The sound of the clock was even more piercing as the noise heightened. Tick tock, tick tock, tick tock. Nothing existed. Time was still. Except for the tick, tock, tick tock, tick tock. I was in this moment as though it were frozen. And so was I. Everything moved, except for that moment, and except for me. I did not stir, but I knew I was drowning; slowly, painfully, languishingly. My life as I had known it was slipping away. And soon I was going to be dead, forever dead, for how would I live again?

Finally, he got off me, and finally, I breathed. I could feel and taste every particle of the free, unobstructed inhalation of air as it entered my mouth and went down my throat, into my lungs and somewhere right to the back of my chest in a place I did not know even existed. My heart was banging as though it would pounce out of my ribcage, and for a few seconds I cowered in the corner of the sofa, pulling my knees to my chest, burying my head in my lap, unable to move, not daring to twitch.

'Now then, now do you see how I feel about you? So, from this day forward, you are mine. You will *always* be mine. This will be our little secret. No one needs to know. What do you say?' I raised my head ever so slightly as he spoke, and I could see that he didn't even look at me as he asked me the question. He talked so casually, so calmly, as though nothing had happened. He leant back, placed his feet on the coffee table, and he idly brushed his hands through his hair. He let out a long, contented sigh, and then leaned forward and pulled out a box of cigarettes and a gold-coloured lighter from the ornate wooden box under the coffee table. He rested back onto the sofa again and slowly lit his cigarette. He smoked it calmly, almost meditatively, closing his eyes with each puff. He blew perfectly round circles of smoke into the air. The circles gently floated up, and then just disappeared. Oh, how I envied those little circles of smoke, for I wished I could do that, I wished I could be one of those circles, and just waft up and disappear.

I could see that he was savouring his cigarette, and so I started to get up slowly, apprehensively. Quietly, and without fuss, I sorted my clothes and slipped my jacket back on. He was still busy enjoying his cigarette, so I picked up the pace, and quickly gathered my books into my bag and headed for the door, but before I could get there, he sprung up and grabbed my right arm, and then the other, and pulled me toward him, squeezing both my arms tightly. He was almost nose-to-nose with me, and I closed my eyes in dread.

'Just one thing before you leave. I mean it. Don't even *think* you can tell anyone about this.' The words were threatening and sadistic, but his tone of voice was much, much worse. If his aim was to frighten me witless, then he was succeeding. 'You see, if you do, I will just deny it. Who is everyone going to believe? The most respected man in the community, who's never done anything but help people, or some little tart who already has a reputation for having boyfriends? Even your mother is more likely to believe me. And think of the shame for your family, the *besti*, especially for her. So, my little beauty, you're not going say anything about this to anybody, are you?' As he spoke the last sentence, he stroked my face and hair with his grubby fingers. I winced as he did so; my skin literally crawled wherever I felt his touch.

'No,' I replied quietly, and then pulled myself away, and ran out of the room and out of the house.

Chapter 5: The Stranger in the Mirror

I SLOWLY CAME OUT of the shower. Still dripping wet, I went and stood in front of the bathroom mirror. I wiped the steam off the mirror with my hand, and stared cautiously at my reflection; the dark brown eyes, now red and puffy after all the crying, stared back at me. They were sad and mournful. They were ashamed and angry. I could see a fire raging in them. Everything else was calm, but the fire burned in those eyes. I couldn't see anyone beautiful in that image. I couldn't even see anyone I recognised. Where was I? That was not me. I looked and looked, searched and searched into those blazing deep chestnut eyes. I wasn't the same girl who had left this house just hours before. I couldn't see *me* when I looked at the reflection. Selina doesn't live here anymore, I thought. She has gone. Perhaps forever.

Chapter 6: Mother's Decision

THE NEXT MORNING, I hurried down with my dirty laundry before anyone else was awake. I loaded the washing machine and switched it on, knowing that no amount of washing powder was going to be able to purify these stained clothes, and no amount of fabric softener was going to rid the stench of last night. I watched the clothes go round and round as I sat at the kitchen table. Round and round went the clothes in the machine. And round and round went the thoughts in my head. Round and round went the flashbacks from yesterday evening.

I could hear a clock ticking away. I looked over at the wall clock; my mum's family had sent it as a gift from Pakistan a few years back. It was a typically *desi*, very gaudy looking clock, with a pale green background and a fancy, bright, gold-coloured frame, with a religious inscription at its centre. I could hear the tick tock, tick tock, tick tock...I went and pulled it off the wall, took the battery out and slid it into the pocket of my fleecy pink dressing gown. I carefully placed the clock back as I had found it. I sat down, put my head in my hands and closed my eyes. Tick tock, tick tock, tick tock. Blast it! I could still hear it. I put my hands over my ears as I leaned onto the dining table, feeling trapped within this echoing prison in my mind, awash with the awful reverberations of yesterday. Tick tock, tick tock, tick tock. 'Go away! Please!' I murmured.

'Who are you talking to?' Mum asked from the hallway. I didn't even hear her come down, I was so pre-occupied with my own thoughts.

'Err, no one mum, I was just going over some of my Shakespeare lines for my exam. You know I'm studying

Hamlet. There's so much to I need to remember,' I replied as she walked in. She didn't have a clue about Hamlet.

'And how come you are up so early? And you have put your washing on!' Mum observed this with a look of amazement plastered all over her face. 'My goodness, what's happened to you today? Where has my Selina gone? Who is this imposter?' If only she knew how those words resonated with me. 'Are you practising for married life? I normally have to yell at you at least twenty times before you bring your washing—' but my mum was unable to finish her sentence as I shot up and suddenly gave her an almighty hug, almost knocking her over. And then I started sobbing. 'Hey, hey, what's wrong?' she asked, trying to prise me off, but I wouldn't budge, and just carried on crying.

She persisted. 'Darling, you are worrying me.'

'It's nothing, I'm just missing dad.' That wasn't a lie, I told myself. It just wasn't the truth either.

'Come, there, there now, we all miss him. Maybe, what with the pressure of your exams, it's all becoming a bit too much for you. The exams will be over soon enough.'

I drew away and went back and sat at the table.

My head felt weary, as though a huge, heavy fog had descended right into it. And I was conscious of a nagging pain, that lay somewhere between my stomach and my chest, like a constantly moving thud of anxiety that was relentless.

'At least you are less worried about your Economics now. You know, I can't thank Brother Zubair enough. He has been a help to us in so many ways; especially when your father died. He was a tower of strength for me. He didn't let me worry about a thing. He took care of absolutely everything; and how wonderful that he should offer to help you. I don't know a finer man than him. And it's not just me who thinks that, everyone in the community feels the same way about him.'

I clenched my hands together tightly at hearing that man's name. But when I noticed the grazes and scratches, I hid my hands under the table. I took a couple of deep breaths to calm my nerves, to make sure my voice would project a very matter of fact tone, before I spoke again.

'Mum, about the Economics lessons. I think we've covered everything now, so I don't need to go to any more study sessions. And to be honest I need the time to revise for my other exams. So can you let aunty Sajda know?'

'Well yes of course I will, if that's what you've agreed with Zubair.'

It had worked. She didn't suspect a thing.

'Thanks, mum.'

'By the way, you know we have fixed the *nikah* day for the 15th of July. And the *walima* down in Birmingham will be exactly a week later. The clothes and jewellery have already arrived, and Sohail's family are delighted with them. I spoke with Sohail's mother last night, and we ironed out a few last-minute details. Your aunty Ruby has so many weird and wonderful things planned for your *walima*. Just wait and see. I'm sorry I can't give you the lavish wedding you deserve. So how about we do your *mehndi* night a couple of days before the *nikah*. You can invite all your friends from school, and there will be the usual families of course. I thought we could book the church hall, I've checked and it's free that day. I thought if we leave a gap, then you can get a rest before the big day? And I am going to collect your wedding outfit from the boutique today; they promised it will have arrived by late afternoon.'

I listened quietly, and it took me a little while before I could gather any energy to protest.

'But mum, you know how I feel about this wedding. Why are you doing this to me?'

'What am I doing? Am I doing anything bad? No parent ever does anything bad to their child, or wishes ill for them. I am securing your future to a family who will always be able to look after you. You will have an absolutely wonderful life. And Sohail is crazy about you. Any fool can see that. It's all sorted.'

I didn't have the will to argue. Not today. This was a battle I would have to save for another time. I was in a traumatised trance that was draining the very life out of me. I still could not believe what had come to pass. My inner feelings were desperately raw, and I physically felt like a sanctum of impurity. And that wasn't all. There was the little matter of my exams. Despite my confused state, there was one thing I was certain of; I had to get those grades and get to university. I had to get away from that man, and try and put what happened behind me. I wasn't going to give up on my dreams.

Chapter 7: Tossing and Turning

I TOOK TWO BUSES to get to a chemist that was some distance away from home, where there was absolutely no chance of anyone who knew me, or my mum, seeing me buy what I needed. On my journey, I started to reminisce, which kept me from dwelling upon the problem at hand, if only for a short while.

Once of the buses went past the old, now largely disused, wool mill that my grandad used to work in. My grandad died only three years before my dad. He was a spritely seventy-nine years old, and I think it was more a case of missing my grandma than that he was too old or terribly ill. He passed away unexpectedly but very peacefully in his sleep one night. My dad was his only son. Since my aunt had lived in Pakistan ever since she had married, when I was only a few years old, and because it was the custom, my grandparents both lived with their son.

I remember, as a child, my grandad used to tell us stories, sometimes in a very animated fashion, about what it was like when he first came to England in the 1960's. I used to listen avidly as he spoke in his mother tongue, and for some reason the tales he told sounded so much better in *Potwari*. Until his wife and children joined him and they bought their first house, he had shared a three-bedroom house with about eight other men. They used to works shifts in the local mills and factories, so the guy who had just done the night shift would hop into the bed of the one who had just vacated it and was leaving for his day work. They actually didn't have a bed each! He said he could speak barely a word of English when he got here, but somehow he managed to land himself a job in local mill in the first week. Back then, he said, whilst there was always that element of society who were out-and-out racist, who didn't want the black or brown people here, there were as many who sensed that immigrants were hard-working and appreciated having employment that paid well in comparison to what they would earn back home. The employers especially appreciated them—"as we would do the *kaam* the *goras* didn't want to do," Grandad would say. He was only paid a few pounds a week, but it was enough for him to have a minimal existence here, and send money back home to his family. I was always fascinated by it, and I used to ask grandfather about it all the time. I remember researching the mill not long after he died. It was a steam-powered, worsted, spinning mill, built in the 1850's. It had three extensions over the years, which was a shame, as now the huge mill with its towering chimney was sitting there, redundant, apart from the section fronting the main road on one side where my bus went by, where there were some retail outlets; carpet shops, kitchen showrooms, that sort of thing. Worsted wool is what's used for tailored clothing, he used to tell me, and woollen wool for jumpers. I had such fond memories of my grandparents who had both lived with us until they passed away, and I especially recalled my grandad's stories with much affection. And my grandma had her moments too, mainly comical ones. Whilst my grandfather picked up English fairly quickly and could hold a decent conversation, in contrast, my grandmother always struggled.

Like the time when I got chicken pox. We must have told her a dozen times that I had *chicken pox*, but somehow she still managed to tell the man at the shop when she went for a loaf of bread that I was feeling terribly unwell and had "coco pops". And the way she could never say "burger" and always referred to it as "gurber", and pizza was always "peesa".

But reflecting upon the past in this dreamy, childlike manner was just a temporary distraction, for nothing could drag me away from thoughts about what had happened for very long. I hadn't told a soul about what Zubair had done, not even Abigail. As it was exam time, we hardly saw each other, and it wasn't the sort of thing I could talk about in a text or phone call. And the longer I left it, the harder it got. So, I decided not to mention it; largely because I couldn't bring myself to talk about it. Abigail had left for Spain as soon as her exams were over, and now my exams had also finished. The exams seemed to have gone surprisingly well considering everything that had been going on. However, it was because of everything that had happened that I was determined to do well.

I tried speaking to my mum about the wedding a couple of times, but I could barely get hold of her, what with her constantly shopping, going out to drop off invites, chatting to the old ladies about what she should and shouldn't do at the *nikah* ceremony. There were all these traditions, and even though she had been through the process once before with Henna, she still liked to consult the elders about all the different rituals. And then there was also the fact that I hadn't been feeling very well. I was exhausted, pretty much all the time. And I felt sick; all the time.

Later that night, when I was sure mum and Adam were asleep, I sat on my bed with the testing stick in my hands, my eyes closed tight. My hands were trembling and I felt a nauseous grumble in the pit of my tummy. I was late. I was never late. Always twenty-five days. Since I was twelve years old my cycle had been every twenty-five days, without exception. I was petrified. I opened my eyes. There it was, the word I had been dreading: 'PREGNANT'.

I could barely believe my eyes. I suddenly felt dizzy. The room seemed to be spinning around me, throwing an array of colours before my eyes; pinks, violets, reds, all darting before me in every direction. I blinked hard, and I tried to ignore the light show, and focus on that word again and again to make sure I was seeing it right. I lobbed the pregnancy testing stick at the wall in a hollow rage, and fell back onto my bed, buried my head under my sequined cushions and fluffy pillows, and cried as quietly as I could. Why was this happening to me?

I couldn't sleep all night. I tossed and flipped, pulled and tugged. My teddies and cushions all ended up in a heap on the floor and the bed sheets were a mess. Thoughts and suppositions trampled through my head, thick and fast. What was I going to do? Who could I talk to? The only person I could ever even think of telling things to was Abigail, but she wasn't back for a while. And I couldn't ring her on holiday to bother her about it, since I hadn't even told her about the rape.

I could get rid of it. I did think about it. After all, I didn't need a permanent reminder of what that beast did to me. But could I? Who would I go and see? Where would I get the money from? And really? Me? Have a termination? No! The truth was that I just couldn't go through with something like that. To abort this baby, however it was conceived, would go against everything I was brought up to believe in—morally, religiously, in every way. It was all very well for me to go on about becoming a human rights lawyer, but what about the baby's right to be born? Could I really kill it, just like that? On the other hand, if I had a baby out of wedlock—that would kill my mum for sure. But it wasn't my fault! He raped me! Would anyone even believe me? Would they believe that he raped me? What if he said I came on to him? I already had a reputation, however unjustly I had acquired it, and he could well play on that. It sounded crazy, but I felt that he was capable of it. I wasn't convinced people would believe me over him. I couldn't even vouch for my own mum let alone the relatives and wider community. And what about the ramifications it would have for my family. There was no way my mum could take the shame and the humiliation that would come with a scandal like that. The community would never let her live it down. The family's *izzat* would be ruined, in tatters. And my father would be tarnished with the same brush even though he wasn't even alive. And I could never bear for anyone to spoil my father's image. And heaven only knows what Zubair's reaction would be. And what about his wife and kids?

After all the ruminating and procrastinating, it seemed there was only one way out of this problem that I could see straight ahead of me; the only way in which to avoid an abortion and not bring dishonour to my family's door. It was obvious really, even if it wasn't entirely palatable; I knew what I had to do.

Chapter 8: Cooking for the in-laws

THE NEXT MORNING, the three of us sat and chatted over breakfast, and I broached the subject of the wedding with my mother, much to her delight, as up until now I hadn't shown the slightest bit of interest, and in fact I had avoided anything relating to it like the plague.

'*Ammee*, I've been thinking about the wedding, and I know you only want what's best for me. So, its fine with me, I will go through with it.'

My mum came hurtling over, and gave me a great big hug, and sat on the chair next to me, almost bursting with joy. It was like music to her ears.

'But I don't want a lot of fuss. And I don't want a henna night. That's not negotiable. I just can't deal with all that stuff. Sitting there like a statue whilst old aunties you've never seen before come and stick henna on your hand, and a lump of *mitai* in your gob, or worse still a whole *forrero rocher!* Ugh! And I don't want too many people at the *nikah*.'

'Oh, my baby, we will do it exactly as you want. I'm so pleased you've had a change of heart. I knew you would come round in the end. But I was thinking about something that we need to address. When you leave your home, at the *rukhsati*, it is customary for your father to give you away to your husband. But obviously your father is no longer with us. So, I was thinking, maybe we could ask someone else who is like a father figure to you to take over that job. I thought someone who has always been there for us, though thick and thin. And so, I think we should ask your Uncle Zubair—'

'No!' I shouted. Both mum and Adam were taken aback with the strength of my reaction, as was clear from the look of astonishment on their faces. They sat there gawping at me; as if to say, did we miss something? Think Selina, think!

'I mean, I can't have anyone try and take the place of my father. My father would be the only person who would befit that role. And as that's not possible, I would like the next best thing. I'd like Adam to do it. Why should some outsider take over when I have a brother who is perfectly capable of doing it; I know he's only fourteen, but that's no big deal. So, what do you say kid?' I asked as I turned toward Adam, whilst nicking a piece of toast from his plate. I could make it as a lawyer yet, I thought.

'If it's okay with you Sis, then it is fine with me. But I'm not a kid; I'm way taller than you now.' Adam was trying his best to stifle a smile that was trying to make an appearance, and I could tell he was feeling chuffed at being asked.

I got up and bent over to try and give him a big kiss to which he retaliated, 'Err, get off me. That's gross. Don't be thinking you can do that to me on your wedding day in front of everyone!'

I noticed the smile on my mum's face as she watched us laughing and messing about. She hadn't smiled in a long time, I thought. At least my marrying Sohail would make my mum happy.

With just over a week to go to the wedding, uncle Ali, aunty Ruby, Sohail and his older sister Tahira came up from Birmingham to go through some last minute preparations. The house was full of noise and chatter, and there was an atmosphere of excitement and anticipation. Henna had also come over for the weekend, with her husband.

My mum had pulled out all the stops, as was to be expected, and though she could ill afford it, she made a lavish meal, which Henna and I were now finishing in the kitchen whilst she sat in the living room chatting to her guests. Everything else for the meal was ready, except the *tandoori*-style chicken drumsticks, which were coming to the end of their roasting time in the oven, and the *rotis*, which I was rolling whilst my sister finished them on the *tawa*. I could never produce them as perfectly round or as fluffy as mum's, but she said I must persist, as it is a critical quality in a Pakistani wife that she makes great *chapattis*. I did often say the man should be equally as good at it, to which she just looked at me curiously. "At least you girls don't have to stick your hand down a burning *tandoor* like I used to back in Pakistan from the age of about ten," she often said as she would stand by me, giving me meticulous instructions on perfecting the task. She said every evening just before dusk, the *tandoors* would be lit all around the village for the evening meal's *chappatis*. The woody, burning smell from the clay ovens would fill the air with an unmistakable smoky aroma. And she reckoned sticking her hands down the *tandoor* meant she never needed to wax her arms!

Henna wasn't entirely happy with the quality of my *rotis*, but deigned to tell me that they were "satisfactory". She always seemed to see the negative side to anything I did, and rarely praised or complimented me. However, her mood seemed to change suddenly to a more pleasant one.

'Listen Selina, I've got some good news, but promise you won't tell mum until I've spoken to her,' said Henna. I looked at her as soon as I had slapped the *roti* dough on the *tawa*. 'I'm pregnant!' she said, looking all gooey-eyed and thrilled at the prospect.

I suddenly felt a little sick and light headed upon hearing her news, and held on to the worktop to steady myself. I swallowed hard to force back down the bile that had climbed up my throat.

'Really? That's amazing news,' I said to her after I had composed myself. 'Congratulations! And my lips are sealed...for now!'

I went and gave my sister a hug, and wished dearly that I had been close enough to Henna to confide in her about my problems. But we had never really been all that attached to each other. If I were to be completely honest, I sensed that Henna had always been a little jealous of me, though she would never admit it. She'd always seemed to begrudge me so many things; my looks, my performance at school, my relationship with our father—everything really. It was only after she had got married and left home that our relationship had improved a little. I think Faisal had been a positive influence on her. Yet, I could still never imagine talking to her about anything intimate.

A few moments later, Sohail walked in with the rattling tray of empty teacups. Henna, sensing she should give us a few moments together, made some excuse about talking to aunty Ruby about the photographer, and promptly left the kitchen. Usually, I would have done anything to avoid spending time alone with him, but today I thought I ought to stay and chat. After all, I had decided that marrying him was the only way out of the quagmire that I found myself in. It was time I became better acquainted with him. Who knows? Perhaps I would grow to like him, maybe even love him one day. After all, my parents had an arranged marriage, and they had managed it.

'So, how are you Selina?' Sohail asked as he put the tray down on the kitchen table. 'Excited about the big day? I must say, you're the most hands-off bride-to-be ever. My mum can't believe her luck, the fact that you're not a bridezilla in the least, and you let her choose and decide everything. She's in her element.'

'Well, I don't really like all that fuss. I just prefer to keep things simple. Not one for pomp and ceremony, me. Anyway, your mum's got impeccable taste, so I totally trust her.'

'I hope you don't mind me saying this, but I'm surprised you agreed to the wedding. I mean, I've liked you for a while. You know that. You're stunning, the most beautiful girl I know. But I've always sensed that you've never been very keen. I was convinced you weren't going to agree to the wedding.

And now that you have consented, I'm excited beyond belief that you are going to become my wife. Nothing in the whole world could make me happier," he said gently, with a soft smile on his face.

For the first time ever, I actually looked at him quite carefully as he spoke. He was a tall man, broad shouldered and well built, and with the medium brown, slightly olive-coloured skin you would expect for a man of Pakistani origin. Truthfully, he was good looking.

'But a little part of me is anxious you may change your mind at the last minute,' he continued. So I have to ask: you are going to go through with it aren't you? Because if you've got any plans to call it off the day before or something, then tell me now. It would be really embarrassing for my family. And I would feel bad for my parents. They've had loads of people contact them with great marriage proposals for me, but I've turned them all down. And that's because I've been smitten with you for ages. I know I'm a few years older than you, but that shouldn't matter, should it? I really do want to marry you. I need to know you feel the same.'

He was dressed in a smart casual designer jeans and a shirt, immaculately turned out as ever, but unlike the brand of his clothes, his face didn't look superficial. It had a genuine quality about it. I had just never bothered looking before. And his words sounded honest, as though they came straight from the heart. As I listened to him talk, an inner guilt crept its way into my head. His words had a genuine edge, and he could not contain the enthusiasm he felt about me, and the wedding to be. I felt bad that I didn't love this man or even care for him particularly. Most of all, I felt bad that I was going to pass off the baby as his. But I had no choice. The die was cast.

'Yes, I do want to marry you.' I answered. 'It's best for all of us; you, me, our parents. I know my mum will be really pleased once we're married, and I want to make her happy. And I know we can be happy together as well. Your parents have done it; my parents did it, why not us? So please, don't fret. I won't be one of those runaway brides or anything like that. On the 15th of July, we will be husband and wife.'

Sohail's brown eyes sparkled, and he unleashed a broad smile when he heard these words. I smiled back at him, feeling I had done enough to reassure him. I only wished that I wouldn't live to regret this decision. But then I knew for sure that the alternative was worse, much worse. So I decided that day, there and then, that I was going to make a real go of my marriage with this man, for better or for worse. Perhaps I really could fall in love with him. I would at least try.

From the minute I agreed to the marriage, the one thought that occupied my mind was: how on earth was I going to get through the wedding night? This was from two perspectives. Since the attack, the mere thought of being touched by a man gave me a creepy sensation and inner dread that I feared would never leave me. How would I be able to endure it? I would need a depth of mental strength the extent to which I had never before been tested. And there was another issue. Even in this day and age, I knew that a man from a family like the Sohail's expected the girls of a family like mine to be pure and virtuous, and there would certainly be questions if this wasn't the case. Boy would I have some explaining to do.

Chapter 9: His farewell speech

IT WAS LATE MORNING on the day of my wedding, and I was ready in my bedroom wearing the pretty *lehnga* dress that my mum had bought for me. I had tried to make contact with Abigail a few times, but we never managed to speak to each other. I missed her, and wished she could be here by my side. I remembered the assurances I had given her, and now thought about how differently things had turned out.

Henna and the other girls abandoned me and ran downstairs to greet the groom and his family, as was customary, adorning them with traditional garlands threaded with colourful fresh flowers, and showering them with fragrant rose petals. I had made sure there were no crimson petals. There were to be pink and yellow ones only. That colour still made me recoil, with its connotations of that chapter of my life that I very much wanted to erase from my memory. The customs of the receiving of the groom and his family would take place first, and then we would all embark on our short journey to the mosque for the wedding ceremony.

Henna would, as was the ritual for the sister of the bride, offer Sohail a drink at the doorstep, and then she would demand money in return before she let him in. She had said that if she was feeling kind, she would give him a glass of mango juice, which I believed to be his favourite, but if she was feeling mean she would give him *rooh afza*. Yuk! I don't think anyone likes the sickly, florally rosy-red *rooh afza*, apart maybe from the oldies born in Pakistan, only because it was the only cordial they were ever given when they were young! I did say to her that mango juice would equal more money. Then, later on in the day, after the wedding ceremony had been conducted, she would sit in the chair next to me, and again seek a further suitably befitting cash payment before vacating the chair to allow him to sit next to his bride. There was another tradition that was popular; that of hiding the groom's shoe, and not giving it back without receiving a goodly sum. However, Henna had made it crystal clear she was not touching any man's shoe, brother-in-law or not. Still, she would profit handsomely from all the other rituals of the day.

All alone in my room, I could hear the *shehnai* playing on the wedding music compilation. There was a constant hum of chitter chatter and laughter coming from downstairs. I looked at myself in the long mirror, all dressed up. The beautician had taken good money, but I was happy that I hadn't been robbed. She had managed to give my face a natural bridal glow, highlighting and contouring my features subtly, just as I had requested. My lips in 'Persian rose', as opposed to the obligatory bright red, and my sultry gold and black eyes completed the look I had wanted of a slightly understated *dulhan* as opposed to one with shovel loads of heavy make-up caked on. In the end, much to my amazement, the dress my mum had ordered for me was actually a work or art. She knew my taste so well, subtle yet eye catching, and not at all blingy. It was a beautiful ivory silk and chiffon mix, embroidered throughout with intricate pale pink thread work and tiny pearly beading. The *kameez* slipped on to me like a glove, the skirt with its ascending flower embroidery was full and long, and my elegant scarf, which had a delicately crafted border all the way around the edges, was pinned to perfection, creating cascades and waterfalls of flowing chiffon. And I loved my jewellery; it was understated, and daintily different, dotted with small, pink gemstones set in gold, unlike the suit of armour you see most Asian brides wearing. Mum's done good, I thought.

I was poised in front of the full-length mirror, gazing at my henna patterns riding up my hands and arms. My *mehndi* artist had designed the patterns just as I had asked; petite flowers, buds and leaves, climbing from my fingers to my elbows in a spellbinding flow, an asymmetrical arrangement that led the eyes mesmerizingly from one end to the other. I'd had to keep the wet henna on for hours to achieve the deep rusty red and orange tones, but the result was spectacular, even if I did end up with a reddish orange patch on my neck where I had plonked my hand in my sleep! Luckily it was to the side of my neck and the jewellery and scarf disguised it well.

As I was admiring the delicate patterns on my skin, I saw the door open in the reflection of the mirror. In walked Zubair. I turned around, twisting my skirt around with me, and instantly my heart started racing at full speed, and my legs were shaking like delicate, windswept leaves.

'What are you doing up here? Get out! Get out or I will scream,' I said to him, trying so hard to raise my voice, but in the end hardly speaking loud enough for him to hear me, let alone anyone else.

'Scream? I can barely hear you myself. You have been avoiding me for weeks. Every time I have come over here, I am told you are out, or unwell, or asleep, or you show your face for two seconds when you bring the tea and then you scarper. And you haven't been round to our house with your mum since I don't know when. This is the first chance I've managed to get to see you alone since that night.'

He looked me up and down with his lingering stare.

'Oh, Selina, you look, ravishing. You are a vision to behold. But tell me, why did you agree to this wedding?'

'That's none of your business.'

'But it is,' he said, coming closer. 'It is every bit my business. You see, we are connected now, and what happened between us, you will always feel it. You will never be free of it. They do say that you never forget your first.' He came closer still until he was right in front of me. 'You are deluding yourself with this marriage rubbish. It's me you want.'

'No it's not. I hate you. Do you hear me; I hate you!'

'Oh come now, is that any way to speak to your first love. It won't last you know. You will be back. It's just a matter of time. And I will be waiting.' He leant over and whispered in my ear, 'You are mine. You'll always be mine Selina. Mine.'

Just then we heard someone calling, mercifully prompting him to dart toward the door, and as he opened it, he found Sajda outside on the landing.

'Zubair, what are you doing up here?' She asked with a degree of surprise that was obvious in her tone of voice. 'Everyone is downstairs.'

He closed the door, but I could make out what they were saying.

'I know; it's just that Selina called me up.' He could lie for England this man. I moved forward and looked through the slight gap in the door.

'Selina? She called you up? Why?' Even his wife could sense that this tall story was odd.

'She was beckoning me from the top of the stairs as I was stood in the hallway downstairs, and I couldn't very well ignore her. I don't know; it's all very peculiar really. I'm more like a father figure to her, or at least I ought to be, but as I told you before, I think she has a bit of a crush on me.'

'I know, you said, and you were right to cancel the rest of the revision sessions, to prevent any awkwardness. Do you think she's okay? I do feel bad for her, missing her dad and everything, but she seems a bit messed up if you ask me. I would say something to her mother, but it's a bit embarrassing really, for them I mean, not you. *You* have nothing to be ashamed of. She's getting married to Sohail today, and yet she has a thing about you, which is ridiculous in itself. Not to mention the reputation she has gathered for herself, it's been all around the neighbourhood for a while, her having had a *gora* boyfriend.' She shook her head seriously in some sort of ritual disgust as she said those last few words.

'Yes, but darling, it's up to us to show a bit of compassion, don't you think? The girl has suffered a terrible loss with her father dying so suddenly. Well, they all have, and I think she has been confused. So she fancies me, or she thinks she does, and maybe she has been messing about with some boy, but perhaps we should put it down to the stress she has been under, and forgive a little indiscretion like that.'

'That's the trouble with you, my darling husband, you're too nice for your own good,' said Sajda, pulling his cheek slightly in jest.

Zubair smiled, and they made their way back downstairs.

I walked away from the door and went over and looked in the mirror again. The last time I had looked at myself this carefully in a mirror was on the night of the rape. I had looked at myself with antipathy, anger, fear and sorrow. I now looked at myself very intently once again. I breathed a heavy sigh. I had to free my mind and body of the incarceration of the brutal attack on that night. I took a deep breath and closed my eyes for a few moments. It was time for new beginnings; time for a fresh start with Sohail. It was time to release myself from the bereavement I had felt of being robbed, of having my innocence ripped away from me, and it was time to let go of the mournful gloom that I had walked around in aimlessly since that night. It was time for the kite to muster up its energy to fly high, and to fly away, for good.

Chapter 10: Bollywood style

WHEN I ENTERED THE ROOM, the guests complimented me on my beautiful appearance, although Henna did not say anything, sadly. Even on my wedding day, she couldn't quite bring herself to do that, although she was happy enough in herself. Surprisingly, Adam, who rarely displayed affection, came over and gave me a hug and told me I looked, "proper nice," and that in front of the guests, too. Sohail looked at me, almost tearfully, as his eyes misted over and his lips displayed a loving smiling. When we were sat together, he whispered to me that he thought I was the most beautiful image he had ever set eyes on. My mum was the proud matriarch, seeing to all her guests, and cooing over me at timely intervals.

When we reached Birmingham, we went to Sohail's parents' house first, where further rituals were performed; I was showered by the young women from Sohail's family with rose petals continuously, as I walked up the enormous driveway and into the house. My father-in-law carried the *Quran,* enclosed in a dark, green, satin cloth, above my head, and Sohail lifted my skirt ever so slightly for me to step nimbly over the threshold. We sat together, and the entertainment began, with onlookers comprised of close family and friends, some standing around, other squashed together on the sofas or perched on the edges. My father-in-law carefully unwrapped the *Quran,* and passed it to me. I opened the Holy Book at the very first page, read the opening page, *Surat Al-Fatihah,* then took a twenty-pound note from my bag and placed it in the page that I had opened. I then gave it back to him, thus passing to him the serious undertaking of ensuring the money reached a worth charity. After my sister-in-law gave me a drink

of milk, for which I rewarded her generously, a different kind
of milk appeared; *haldi* milk. A ring was hidden in this large
metal bowl of milk coloured with turmeric powder, lurking
somewhere at the bottom of the bright yellow liquid. The idea
was that the bride and groom would search for the ring, and
whoever plucked it out would be the more dominant in the
relationship. I had seen this done dozens of times, and it was
always the bride. When Sohail whipped it out, holding it up
high in response to the cheers and laughter that erupted
around us, I felt a tingling anxiety crawl through me. I smiled
as I looked at him, and I knew it was just a silly inconsequential
bit of fun. Nevertheless, it unnerved me.

After all the guests had departed from his parents' home,
Sohail and I left to go to his house. We were alone.

I dreaded and feared the very worst, for I knew that Sohail
would discover I wasn't a virgin, and he would certainly ask
questions. The injustice of it all angered me. No one would
ever question him about his sexuality, but only because he was
a man. As I was a girl, I seemed to be answerable if I didn't
turn out to be as pure as the driven snow. I had tried to
mentally prepare myself for the worst-case scenario. The
feeling of not wanting to be touched remained, although Sohail
was so much more thoughtful than I could have imagined. He
took me through it all gently, at my pace, and I didn't feel
pressured or rushed. He treated me delicately, with the lightest
of caresses and the softest of kisses, and the entire experience
of my wedding night was a world away from the traumatic
ordeal that I had suffered at the hands of Zubair. In the end,
unbelievably, luck was on my side, as the pregnancy had caused
some timely spotting, and this mercifully got me past the
virginity obstacle. It was such a relief.

On the day of the *walima*, exactly a week later, from the
moment I awoke, amidst all the hustle and bustle, a couple of
issues had preoccupied my mind, as I was daunted by the
enormity of the day ahead. The beauticians busily worked their

magic. The hairdresser fussed over and teased every strand of hair into place with every type of hair product and hairpin imaginable. The *mehndi* artist delicately went over my now somewhat faded henna with the glitter art that gave it new life, as the climbing, flowery patterns on my hands and arms now sparkled. But despite all this commotion, my mind quietly ticked away. Firstly, but not really all that importantly, how was I going to make it down the red carpet aisle without tripping? Secondly, and equally trivially, would I be able to cut the cake and feed it to Sohail, and be fed a piece in return without turning a beet-root red, knowing that six hundred plus pairs of eyes were going to be on me? But finally, having felt guilty since before I married him a week ago about the secret I was harbouring, and with my anxiety over my guilt ever increasing, how would I cope with the day at all? But cope I must, I told myself. There was no hiding place. All I *wanted* to do was put on my cosiest pyjamas, grab a cup of tea and a whole pack of lemon puffs and catch up on East Enders. But want never got, I told myself.

As I had anticipated, the *walima* had been all glitz and glamour, with my in-laws relishing the opportunity to show off their money in the best way possible--lavishing it on their only son, of course. They were typical Asians in that sense, although quite untraditional and modern in other ways. Spending their wealth on their son and letting the world see it gave them great satisfaction. They had booked a large, very stylish, out-of-town country manor hotel, hosting six hundred guests in an enormously lavish, stately-looking hall, almost palatial in its proportions; the wooden floors gleamed in their own glow of splendour, and the majesty of the tall, original, wood-framed windows, dressed with ostentatious gold swags and tails, exuded the luxury of a bygone era. All of this overlooked immaculately mowed, green lawns with lush fields beyond. There was a striking lake in the distance complete with white swans floating along and ample car parking space, which always impressed the guests.

There was a story behind my mother-in-law's insistence on generous, on site car parking. She recalled being invited to the wedding of the son of some millionaire friends of theirs last year, to the Banqueting Suite at the National Indoor Arena; an expensive enough venue, and therefore impressive in that sense, but located in the heart of Birmingham City Centre. So cars had to be parked in the multi-storey car parks nearby. On this occasion there were various other events going on at the NIA and the Symphony Hall, and so they had to park a bit further afield than they would have liked. Aunty Ruby was wearing her very high-heeled designer sandals, which she just had to mention she had bought from Harvey Nics, and by the time they reached the wedding, her feet were covered in blisters and were bleeding. She had to send uncle Ali out to a shop to find plasters, and he missed most of the meal! So it turned out that they both had a miserable evening, and all because of the lack of on-site car parking.

The guests were fully assembled and waiting pensively, having eaten their way through the contents of the gold organza-favour bags containing the sweets, nuts, chocolates, and *supari*, and having nibbled on the pineapple chunks, grapes, and strawberries from the edible table fruit decoration.

Sohail and I walked in with the extremely loud and vibrant *dhol* players, and following not long behind us were the exuberant Bollywood-style dancers. The music blared loudly and they danced with boundless energy and effortless synchronisation. The tables were sumptuously decorated to match my star-studded dress of burgundy, gold and cream colours. It must have had a thousand crystals, pearls and beads hand sewn onto to it, which was obviously why it weighed a ton and cost a small fortune. I could buy a brand new car for that much, I thought, only I couldn't drive yet. It was a real effort to drag the damn thing along, and it was so cumbersome that I thought I might actually fall over. Imagine that! Knowing my luck, someone would catch it on their phone, and it would go viral. My jewellery was no less dramatic or weighty. The earrings were so large that I was sure my ears would split by the end of the day. But that I could cope with. It was the *amount* of jewellery I had on that was the problem; earrings, a sweeping, five-tiered necklace that started at my neck and ended around my tummy, *chumar, tikka*, two dozen bangles, a five-ringed bracelet...I felt like I was being crushed. I wasn't keen on the nose ring, but acquiesced in the end.

We nervously walked down the red carpet, which was flanked either side at timely intervals with ivory pillars that were meticulously adorned with fresh flowers, largely a mix of cream- and crimson-coloured roses. I could not escape that damn colour; it was everywhere. Perhaps I should have taken more interest in the colour scheme, I thought to myself, as we walked down with hundreds of eyes on us, watching our every step. My mum and the rest of my family sat at the head table, gazing toward us as we came down, and they looked happy and proud. We daintily stepped onto the stage in a blaze of colour, music and dance. It was just as my mother-in-law had wanted it, and planned it—like a Bollywood blockbuster movie scene. It's as though she had directed some epic film scene, and wanted it to look as though it were Salman Khan and Katrina Kaif gliding down, amidst the colourful splendour of the backing dancers, and dramatic sounds and rhythms of the musicians. And she knew, as she carefully surveyed the faces around the hall, taking her time and soaking in the atmosphere, she knew that she had done a grand job. The sly smile on her face said it all. She could not have looked smugger even if she had tried with all her might. In her mind, it was a mission accomplished, as the other families who sat watching in amazement would have to go some to beat this. She relished the look on the numerous aunty *ji's* faces as they wondered how they were going to outdo Ruby's efforts on their son or daughter's wedding day. She achieved the reaction in peoples' faces that she had longed to see; awe, amazement, jealousy. Others turned away from the unmistakable look of satisfaction and conceit on my mother-in-law's face.

Chapter 11: Four Oaks

I RECEIVED A PHONE CALL from Abigail. I hadn't managed to speak to her since I had moved down. I'd changed my phone, and the number, and it had taken her a while to get my new number from my mum. She'd achieved the grades to go to Southampton University to do History as she had wanted. She sounded really excited. She was now going to start gearing up for her big move. I was pleased for her. Inevitably, the issue of my marriage cropped up as soon as all the niceties were over.

'Selina, I can't believe you went ahead with the wedding. What on earth happened girl? Last time we spoke about this, you were adamant that you weren't going to go ahead with it. You were going to speak to your mum and put a stop to it all. What went wrong? What changed?' she asked me vociferously.

I thought, just for a split second, of telling her about the rape, but in all honesty, I just didn't want to talk about it, I didn't want to think about it, I didn't want to dredge it all up again. It was in the past, and that's where it was going to stay, now that I had moved on to a new phase in my life. Things were pretty good down here, and I was looking forward to having the baby. The baby would be that one person, the one good thing that would come out of this horrid mess; the one human being that I would be able to call my own, completely and without reservation. The one person that I could love unconditionally, and who would love me back in the same selfless way. So, I decided not to revisit that most tumultuous episode of my young existence that I would obliterate, if only I could.

'You know what Abigail, you were right, the pressure just became too much, and I buckled under the weight of it all. It

was really hard for me. My mum has had such an awful time
recently with my dad passing away. So I went through with it,
mainly to make my mum happy. But do you know what, it has
actually all worked out just fine. I really misjudged Sohail. He's
a lovely man. I couldn't ask for a better husband.'

So we left it at that. And I think there was a certain
inevitability that we would probably drift apart now that we
were no longer going to see each other very often, if at all.

As I put the phone down, Sohail walked into the kitchen.

'Good morning, gorgeous wife,' he declared, as he came
over and wrapped his arms around me.

'Good morning yourself! Although it's not going to be
morning for much longer. I know it's Saturday, but someone
had a good lie-in.'

'That's because you kept me awake for half the night,' he
said, squeezing me tightly against him. He was still very much
in the honeymoon phase.

'It takes two to tango, you know. Anyway, tell me, what do
you want for breakfast?'

'No, you go sit down. I'll make the food. You do enough
cooking all week,' he replied. He then changed his voice to a
terrible French accent. 'So, what will it be, Madam? A full
English fry-up with omelette, or a continental breakfast of
croissants and pain-au-chocolat?'

'What do you think?'

'Continental breakfast coming right up madam!'

The Ali family had a thriving accountancy practice. In
addition to Sohail and uncle Ali, their mum also worked there
full-time. We all lived in the prestigious, exclusive Four Oaks
estate in Sutton Coldfield, but the office was on the other side
of Birmingham, in Moseley. Sohail and I lived in a lovely,
detached four-bedroom house, far too big for just the two of
us, and his parents lived in an even bigger house a few minutes'
walk away. I didn't see my-sister-in-law very often, as she lived
in Coventry. So I spent most of the day alone, and I couldn't

even drive yet. Four Oaks Estate was very posh, and very quiet. There were leafy green, wide roads, and grand houses, but above all it was very, very quiet, bar the odd running fitness freak. There were no shops nearby, and it was certainly nothing like the area I had grown up in. Here, you had to pretty much walk for ten minutes before you reached your neighbour, and there was no local grocery store or take away. This was in stark contrast to the hustle and bustle that I had known since I was born, where there were streets filled with kids on their bikes and trikes, and the nearby park packed on sunny days with would-be footballers and cricketers, and the local shopping parade just a couple of minutes' walk away was bursting with all manner of retailers from the chicken shop to the fabric store to the 24-carat gold jewellers. I did catch the train into the city centre occasionally to do the odd bit of shopping, but I couldn't even manage one proper turn of the Bull Ring shopping centre without coming back worn out. I never was a big shopper anyway, and even the 'no limits' credit card given to me by my husband couldn't tempt me.

The house, I had to admit, was stunning; it was constructed in a tasteful, modern design and it was spacious, light and airy. It had solid, dark, oak floors and contrasting dark and pale leather furnishings. There were luxurious Persian rugs dotted around the house, and many attractive paintings and showpieces. I only disliked one thing—the pendulum clock in the front reception room. I wished it wasn't there, but it looked like a one-off designer piece of clockwork art, and no doubt it must have cost a pretty penny, so I didn't dare suggest getting rid of it.

I especially enjoyed sitting in the lounge overlooking the pretty back garden, which was abundantly stocked with a dazzling array of flowers, ferns and foliage, and there was a well-placed, eye-catching fountain that sparkled in the sun, and sounded like bliss. Sohail had already arranged for a gardener who came every week, and a cleaner who came twice a week.

The ironing was collected and delivered immaculately pressed, and there was only so much cooking I could do.

We were a few weeks into the marriage, and I had to say, quite to my surprise, Sohail and I had been getting on very well with each other, pretty much since day one. And as a bonus, things were good with his family too. They weren't actually the interfering type, and so weren't typical Pakistani in-laws in that sense. We didn't all live together, and mum was right, that did help. We often went round to his mum and dad's place, or should I say mini-mansion, but then always came back to our own home, and so it was just the two of us, without any interference or interruptions, and we were bonding far better than I had dared to even imagine. It wasn't possible to go on honeymoon straight away because of Sohail's workload at the office, and in any event, we thought it would be better to go away during the Christmas and New Year break, when he had some proper time off. Nevertheless, we enjoyed each other's company; going out for meals, going to the movies, dinners at his parents' house every weekend, long drives to the country. We had fun together, which had been an unforeseen but pleasant revelation. He was always very busy Monday to Friday with his job, but he was all mine at the weekends, and I hadn't expected that we would rub along so well. He was actually kind and considerate to me. He told me he loved me, and we grew as a couple. We laughed and joked, and I was bowled over by the fact that I actually liked him. I still found the act of lovemaking somewhat awkward, even though Sohail was a world away from Zubair. But I was careful to keep these feelings of awkwardness to myself. I had been raped, and I had to accept that the negative impact of such a disturbing event would always stay with me to some degree. I would have to learn to manage it.

I settled into life with him in a way I could not have imagined. And it wasn't just about grand gestures and sentiments. The ordinary was good, too. Even just lying on the sofa together and watching our favourite television show was cool. It felt normal. And it felt comfortable. And soon it began to feel like home, my home, our home.

Of course, I missed my mum and brother, they phoned or face-timed nearly every day, and I kept in touch with Henna as well. My mum didn't drive, so she couldn't come down very much, as it took her and Adam a few hours and two trains to reach us, and it was even longer on the coach. But Sohail drove me up to see them every couple of weeks. Ideally, I would have loved to have been closer to them, but despite this, I did get a blow-by-blow account from my mum on the phone of every little thing that had, or indeed had not, happened, and if I was lucky, then Adam came on the phone to say a few words, most of which were hard to make out as he spoke in some alien, teenage way, where the words just seem to smudge into one long one that you couldn't fathom, or you got a grunt at best.

I hadn't expected all that much from married life, given the circumstances in which I had quickly decided to marry, but that said, I was very content with my situation. I was a tad bored when Sohail wasn't around, but that wasn't really much of a hardship. My life had funnelled its way into a path that was far less rocky than I had dared to wish. I wasn't expecting a bed of roses, but if I was to tell the truth, without reservation, then I would have to say that I was now living in an altogether different world that had little in it to trouble or annoy me.

Chapter 12: The news is delivered

I RECEIVED MY 'A' LEVEL RESULTS, and somehow I had done it. I had achieved my three 'A's, which I had strived so hard for, and Birmingham University immediately firmed their offer. So, Sohail and his parents thought we should go out and celebrate my achievements.

I was seated with my husband and his parents, a little uncomfortably—not because of the company, but more because we were in a terribly swanky, and apparently award-winning restaurant, which served the likes of cumin and chilli infused rabbit *tikka* instead of the usual chicken variety, and duck cooked with ginger and pomegranate molasses replacing the more well-known and traditional *jalfrezis* or *karahis* of this world, dishes I was much more accustomed to. I missed my mum's home cooking. No amount of fine dining could ever compare to her dishes, which tasted of that unique combination of years of heritage and experience infused with the love that only a mother can impart into the food she prepares for her children. Whilst I sat there, outwardly celebrating my success with my new family, I was secretly thinking to myself about how I would have to delay university because of the baby. It was whilst I sat there that I decided it was now time to think about mentioning the pregnancy to him, and promised myself I would do it—I would tell him. The following day.

It was now the 18th of August, the day I was going to give my husband the news. It had been five weeks since our wedding. Today seemed like a good day, I thought, as I sat in the back garden. It was a shiny, warm day; the sky was a beautiful, pure blue overhead, speckled with just the odd pieces of thin, streaky white cloud. The air smelt clean and light, with just a hint of jasmine drifting around. The drooping branches of the handsome weeping willow at the bottom of the garden swayed to and fro ever so slightly as they caught the breeze. As I sat sipping a sparkly glass of lemonade in the garden, I drifted into thoughts about my life before and since my time here. My life had been a rollercoaster ride since my dad had passed away; one of those crazy hideous ones that takes you through unexpected dips and turns and then flips you upside down. But things were now quite settled, and it felt more like I was travelling in a gently moving Ferris wheel. The carriage was comfortable, and whilst there were little ups and downs, on the whole, the journey was smooth, and whenever I was at the top, the view was pretty good.

I turned my mind to the present and sat right back in my chair in the garden and closed my eyes, listening to the birds tweeting in the background. I concluded, as if to reassure myself, that this was definitely a good day to give Sohail the news. So that's what I did—in the evening, straight after dinner as we settled down on the sofa after we had eaten.

'Sohail, I've got some something to tell you.'

'You have? What is it?' he asked casually, as he switched the television on to the sports channel.

'Well, I may as well come straight out with it. I'm pregnant.'

As soon as I had uttered the words, Sohail erupted into a tizz of excitement. He quickly switched the television off and turned to look at me, he grabbed both my hands into his. His wide smile lit up his face, and his eyes twinkled with delight.

'That's fantastic news! I can't believe it. I'm so thrilled! Oh my God, I'm going to be a dad!' He said, now waving his arms around in the air, and then flinging them around me. He acted and sounded genuinely ecstatic, and I felt genuinely guilty. I was starting to worry that the guilt I felt would consume me, and worse still, that it would begin to show on my face.

'Yes, but its early days yet,' I said, trying to calm him down a little, not that it did much good.

'I know, but I'm so excited. I mean, I didn't think that you would get pregnant so soon, like pretty much straight away by the looks of it. I've got to tell mum and dad. Please, can we?' Sohail asked, like a schoolboy asking for a sweet at the shop.

'Well, I suppose so. Go on then. But that means I will have to tell my mum as well. We can't tell one side and not the other. That's asking for trouble!'

Both sides of the family were absolutely delighted. Mum was over the moon when I'd called her with the news. Now she had not only one, but two grandchildren coming. 'It's like the buses,' she said to me. 'You wait ages for one, then two come at once!' She was ecstatic.

I had managed to go see the doctor on my own. Sohail was supposed to come with me, but I had secretly made a different appointment. So I phoned him at work and claimed that the surgery had rung and there had been a mix up with the appointments, and I had to go in straight away that morning, or else it would be a while before I got another appointment. It was believable enough, but I still hated myself for lying like that, for being so sly and underhanded. But I didn't see that I had much option. Things were as they were, and I had to just try and get through these awkward hurdles, one at a time.

I was finishing my breakfast at the island in the kitchen a couple of weeks later when Sohail brought the post through. He didn't bother opening it and left it with me as he rushed off, already late for work. My appointment for the scan had arrived. Sohail had noticed the hospital stamp on the letter as he had handed it to me, as was evident from our conversation later in the day.

'Was that the appointment for the scan that arrived this morning?' he asked over dinner. I put my fork down, resigned to the fact that I had eaten enough. I was no longer enjoying the chicken on my plate. Lately, I'd come to dislike anything meaty, and any dish that was even a little bit spicy. Both just made me wretch. None of this was like me at all, as I usually loved to eat both, in fact the hotter the better normally. Now I couldn't stand the sight, smell or taste of chillies or turmeric or cumin. I wondered if I was going to feel like this for the whole of the pregnancy. Or worse still, feel like this even after the baby was born!

I turned my mind to Sohail's question. 'Yes, yes it was.' I replied a little nervously, feeling the butterflies in my tummy. I had to make sure, in any which way I could, that he didn't come to the scan.

'When is it? Obviously I'm going to come as well,' he said, with excitement practically singing from his words and brimming from the smile on his face. His smile could not have been broader. And unlike me, he was clearly enjoying my chicken *tikka masala* curry and *pilau* rice, which he was wolfing down after a long day at work.

'It's on the 25th of September. I can go on my own if you don't have time. It's not a problem.' I really wanted to avoid his coming to the scan at any cost. It was going to be tricky but I had to do it. I would deal with the baby coming early when it happened. I had to overcome this obstacle first.

'No,' he said, putting his fork down to give me his full attention, 'you went for your initial appointment at the surgery on your own, and I felt bad. So I'm going to make sure there is no way I am missing this, no matter what. I'm going to be there for you, and the baby, every step of the way. I'm so excited, I literally can't wait!' He reached over and placed his hand on mine assuredly.

My stomach gurgled, and I'm sure this was more as a result of my nervousness than anything else. I had to ensure that he didn't make it to that scan, somehow, some way, any which way I could. But I hadn't the faintest how I was going to stop him. He was on a mission to be involved with the pregnancy every single step of the way. I started to pray in my mind for a miracle.

Chapter 13: The silence

ABOUT A WEEK BEFORE THE DATE of the scan, Sohail came home looking despondent and miserable, dragging his heels, his face looking like he was someone who had just won a million-pound lottery ticket and then promptly lost it. He walked into the bedroom, all doom and gloom, and started loosening his tie. I was pottering around the room rearranging the contents of a few drawers, and noticed he looked very downbeat. I stopped what I was doing, flung a bunch of his ties over the back of the chair by the dressing table, and came over and sat with him on the bed.

'What's wrong?' I asked him, sensing he was obviously disgruntled about something.

'You're not going to like this. Honest to God, I'm so annoyed. It's the scan. I can't make it. I completely forgot that ages ago, mum and dad booked a week's holiday for themselves in September, so they're going to be away then, sunning themselves in Oman, would you believe. Even then, it wouldn't matter because the staff can look after things, but we've got this really important potential client booked in that day, and I have to see him. He is too big a deal for me not to be there, not to mention that mum and dad would kill me. I would rearrange it but he's flying in from abroad especially, so I can't. I'm so sorry; I really wanted to come with you. I just really, really wanted to see the image of our little baby in the monitor.'

He leaned over and gave me a warm hug, and I rested my head on his shoulder, inhaling his familiar, comforting scent. His strong, muscular arms felt warm, and safe. Solace; the shroud of his arms felt like solace. I slowly closed my eyes. Secretly, and somewhat contritely, I breathed a vast sigh of relief that he wasn't coming to the scan. It was as if, for a change, my prayers had been truly answered. I felt bad for the deceit, but was so very grateful for the good hand that fate had dealt me, for once.

'Honestly Sohail, it's fine,' I said, pulling my head back to look at him, feeling regretful as I gazed into his eyes. He didn't deserve this deception, and I felt completely rotten about my duplicitous behaviour. 'Don't feel bad. Really, it's okay. I will be absolutely fine. And you know I will bring the pictures back for you so you will still be able to see the baby. From what I hear, there's just a lot of waiting around anyway. The scan itself only takes a couple of minutes. The most important bit is the photo of the scan which I won't forget to ask for.'

He shrugged his shoulders slightly and then gave me a quick kiss, which turned into a much longer one.

'Okay,' he said, as he pulled away, 'it will have to do, as I don't really have much of a choice, do I? But I want you to take a photo of the image the second you have it in your hand and send it to me on my phone. I won't be able to wait until the evening.'

'Of course I will,' I replied as he hugged me. I reciprocated and embraced him even tighter, feeling safe in his arms. Safe....in a man's arms. That's something I never thought I would ever feel after what had happened to me. I was now so far away from that girl who just a few months ago hadn't even given a second look to this man; a man who clearly loved me, and who I now was beginning to trust, and perhaps even love a little.

The day of the scan came, after what seemed like forever, and I called a taxi to get to the hospital in good time. I had been told to drink loads of water, so I was dying for a wee already. Goodness knows how I would survive until my appointment time. And the speed bumps by the hospital didn't help.

I checked myself in and was told to sit in the waiting area. The ante-natal clinic was very busy, as expectant mums with varying sizes of bumps sat and waited to be called. Most of them had their partners by their side, so I guess I must have stood out a bit, just like a couple of others who were there alone. So I, like the other two loners, sat down and waited quietly, whilst the dozen or more couples chatted away to each other. After what seemed like another piece of eternity, but was in fact exactly twenty-five minutes, as I had watched the clock incessantly, I was called through to go down a corridor and was told to sit in another waiting area, just outside the sonographer's room. More waiting. I was told that I had to have a full bladder to make sure the baby would be clearly seen, but I was fit to burst and was sure I was going to wet myself imminently. To stop myself from thinking about needing the toilet, I kept reading the posters about the do's and don'ts of pregnancy, and about the virtues of breastfeeding over formula milk, and how dads can help their partners, and I read them again and again, until I swore I could repeat the contents off by heart. I wish I had brought a book or magazine to read.

At last, I was called in. With some difficulty, trying not to have an accident as by now I felt sure I was about to explode, I got onto the bed, and tried to get "comfortable". The sonographer was a tall, slim lady. She had a long, thin face and wavy dark brown hair, and she talked very quietly. She asked me how I was, and she then went on and explained the procedure. All I could think was "get on with it woman!" She placed the icy, cool gel on my tummy, which made me jump a bit. Just as she was about to get started, there was a knock on the door, much to my annoyance as I just wanted this over with so I could run to the loo. I had never in my life been so desperate to go to the toilet.

The sonographer went to the door and spoke to another lady. She waited for a few moments and then started to let someone in.

My jaw just dropped. I couldn't believe it. It was Sohail.

'Like I said to your colleague, I'm really sorry I'm late, but I am the father, and I didn't want to miss it,' he said to the sonographer.

'That's okay,' she replied. 'Dads are always very welcome. Please, come on in and take a seat here next to your wife.'

'Surprised to see me!' Sohail said to me with jazz hands and a big grin on his face. He was like the cat that got the cream.

What have you done Sohail? I thought to myself. What on earth have you done? A creepy feeling overcame me. This could not end well. Suddenly the air in the room felt dry and coarse. An innate fear started to grab my throat, as if it would choke me there and then. I gave a little cough, as though that would make the feeling vanish. If only.

'Yes, of course I'm surprised. You told me you weren't coming, I thought you had an important client, or something,' I responded, trying to give an air of composure, hoping the nervousness in my voice wouldn't be apparent.

'I did, but can you believe it, he telephoned me just about an hour ago saying he couldn't make it today, and could he come in tomorrow instead. So as soon as he put the phone down I pegged it across here like grease lightning. I'm sure I got flashed by a speed camera or two. But it looks like I just made it in time, thank God.'

He came and sat on the chair beside me and held my hand. I was sure it was really sweaty by now, as my anxiety continued to grow. I felt as though the walls were closing in, and that I might stop breathing soon. A feeling of foreboding was beginning to overtake me.

We both watched intently as the sonographer carried out her work without saying anything. She seemed a little perplexed. She looked at the pregnancy notes, and back up at the screen, and repeated this action twice. She's spotted it, I thought to myself. Of course, she has. She wouldn't be much good at her job if she hadn't. If only Sohail had not turned up. My lying and deception were all about to unravel, right here, right this very minute. It was like a high-speed train hurtling along the track that I just couldn't stop. I couldn't prevent the inevitable. How did I ever even think that I would get away with it?

'Is there something wrong?' Sohail asked, looking concerned that there may be some problem with the baby. I knew full well what was wrong, and was dreading what she was going to say next.

'Mrs Ali, according to the dates you have given to your midwife, you think you are about eleven and a half weeks pregnant. But looking at the scan, you appear to be around fifteen to sixteen weeks into your pregnancy.'

Sohail stared at the sonographer in utter disbelief. He let go of my hand, sat up straight and blinked a few times.

'Are you sure?' Sohail asked with a little hesitation. He then looked at me. I could feel a burning sensation crawling up my neck and cheeks. I turned my face away, unable to look at him.

'Absolutely; there's not much doubt about that, I can assure you. I wonder, perhaps you got your dates mixed up? Believe it or not, it happens often. But other than that, everything is fine. The baby looks very healthy, and generally speaking, all is well. There is nothing to be concerned about, the growth and development are all okay,' the sonographer finished with a slightly laboured smile, just before she handed the photos of the scan image to Sohail. I immediately ran to the toilet as soon as it was all over.

We walked out of the hospital in complete silence. I didn't know what to do. Should I say something? No, I concluded—not here, and not in the car. I should wait until we get home, I thought.

Sohail didn't speak for the entire journey back to the house. In fact, he hadn't uttered a word since we had left the sonographer's room. He had placed the scan photo in my lap and just started driving. I looked at the photo for a couple of seconds, and I wanted to carry on looking at it, to coo over it, to take my time to spot the arms and legs, but in the circumstances

I thought it wise not to, and I placed the photo carefully into my handbag. The car ride back home was stiflingly silent, and uneasy. And quick, as he put his foot down like a nutter.

Sohail drove abruptly onto the driveway. I got out of the car, expecting him to follow, but without saying a word he reversed his Mercedes SLK and drove away, the gravel on the driveway flicking up high as he burned the rubber to speed off in a hurry.

I stood in the driveway for just a minute or so, looking at nothing in particular, just standing there. Then I gazed up at the sky, and saw that the rain clouds were gathering. The gloom in the sky mirrored the darkness inside of me; as the grey clouds hurried to congregate together above me, so the negative thoughts flooded into my mind and swirled around in there with some speed. I entered the house feeling desolate, and went and sat on the bottom step of the stairs in the hallway. And I cried. My nerves were a tangled mess, and I wondered to myself how I was going to summon the courage to face this. How was I going to face yet another disaster in my life? How was I going to even try to justify myself to this man? I would have to tell him the truth, nothing else was going to do here. But would he be able to understand? Would he ever be able to love me, and to love this child? Would he ever forgive me?

Chapter 14: The Confrontation

SOHAIL RETURNED at around midnight. I had been waiting in the kitchen with the door firmly closed, as I couldn't bear the tick tock, tick-tock of the modern pendulum clock; very arty it was, tall and slim, made almost entirely of glass, and it had a long thin silver pendulum. As the noise travelled from the front room in which it hung, it seemed louder than it actually was, especially in the quiet of the evening.

I suddenly flinched. Even with the kitchen door closed tight, I heard the front door loudly bang shut as he entered the house. I opened the kitchen door, and saw his face. He looked mad. Really mad. His usually flawless skin on his face seemed to be a patchy red, and his eyes looked dark and almost threatening.

'Sohail, we need to talk.' I said, as he walked past me and into the kitchen

'Oh, we need to talk, do we? You reckon, do you?' Sohail snapped back at me as he went across the kitchen for a drink from the fridge. He grabbed a carton of orange juice and slammed the door shut, making me jump once again.

I went and stood by the island, feeling a little scared, unable to anticipate what was coming next, for I had never before seen him remotely annoyed, let alone full-on angry.

He finished his drink and leaned against the worktop, which was over on the other side of the gleaming, granite-topped island. He looked straight at me, in a way I had never seen him look at me before. How I now longed for the old Sohail back, the way his eyes would light up first thing in the morning when he woke up next to me, and last thing at night when we made love or laughed and joked during our pillow

talk. This was far, far away from those gentle, tender eyes full
of warmth and serenity. These eyes looked incensed, indignant.
These eyes were ablaze with hate and abhorrence.

'So, whose filth are you carrying?' He said it in the most
venomous, derogatory tone, with a slight nod of the head. He
had already made his mind up, without even having listened to
a word I might have to say. There was no reservation of
judgement in his words or mannerism. It was an open and
shut case by the looks of it.

'It's not like that, I promise you.' It was going to be an
uphill struggle; I was sure of it.

'Let me guess, you messed around, you got yourself up the
duff, your boyfriend ran a mile, so you thought, "I know what.
I'll palm it off as Sohail's. He's gullible enough"—did you
seriously think I was never going to find out? How *stupid* do
you think I am? And how *pathetic* are you? You've always gone
around acting all righteous, all holier-than-thou, thinking you're
better than everyone else. I mean, you never used to give me
the time of day, did you? Always acting all high and mighty;
and all along, you've been nothing but a two-bit slapper. Mind
you, we did hear of a rumour about you and some boy, but we
ignored it, thinking it was just idle gossip. We could never quite
believe that one of uncle Hussain's daughters would behave in
such a crass, cheap way. How wrong we were; and how wrong
I was. You're nothing more than a common whore!'

My tears just started dripping from my eyes, flowing down
my hot cheeks and leaving streaks of watery mascara behind. I
didn't expect to feel so wounded. It felt like he had ripped my
heart out, stamped on it, and kicked it to one side when he said
the things he did.

He ignored my tears and walked out of the kitchen to go
up the stairs. I instinctively turned and followed him. I had to
explain everything to him. He had to give me the opportunity
to do that, to make him understand, and at least hear me out,
and then he could deliver his judgement. He couldn't just say

such horrid things, and make completely false accusations without at least listening to my defence.

Try as I did, I was unable to control my tears or sense of dread as I marched right on behind him, talking, or rather babbling almost incoherently as I went.

'Please, Sohail, look here, come on, listen to me, it wasn't my fault. I panicked and didn't know what to do. I didn't mean to hurt you, honestly.'

I followed him up the stairs, and as we reached the top few steps, I grabbed his arm, sobbing away, but nevertheless desperately trying to explain to him what had actually happened. But he was unmoved, and not interested in my seemingly hideous attempt to actually try and justify my heinous act.

'Of course it wasn't your fault, it was an immaculate conception. What sort of a fool do you take me for? Now let go of me!'

'Please, please, believe me,' I stuttered, hanging onto his sleeve, 'oh please, you have to. I don't have anyone else, please! I was—'

But I never finished my sentence. I didn't say another word. He pushed me away with some force. I lost my footing, and fell all the way down the staircase. Three seconds later I was in a heap at the bottom of the stairs. And then, I didn't remember anything until I woke up the next day.

Chapter 15: My head hurts

'SO, HOW ARE YOU THIS MORNING? Looks like you are still a bit groggy. Well, it's to be expected. Mrs Ali, you've had rather a nasty experience, and of course it's going to be a shock to the system. But not to worry, you'll soon be right as rain.'

I started to open my eyes, slowly. I could smell disinfectant. Or was it bleach? I had such a banging headache, and I felt so lost. Everything was so hazy, and sort of dreary. As I focused my gaze a little, and as my vision became a tad clearer, I saw that a nurse was stood by me. She was petite, with a smooth, straight ginger bob, and she had a very smiley face, as was evident from the smile lines that framed her mouth. She had very bright, red lipstick on. I could only really see the lips. She stood patiently by me, perhaps waiting for a response to her earlier question. But I had forgotten her question. I had questions of my own.

'Where am I? What's happening? What time is it?' I asked. Then I realised that my throat felt really sore, and my voice was very croaky. It was actually quite a strain to speak.

'You're at the Women's Hospital,' the nurse told me, as she took my temperature and then placed the black strap around my arm to take my blood pressure. 'You came in just after midnight last night. And it's now seven o'clock in the morning. Breakfast will be here soon, although I don't think you're up to it yet. I think you will be on the drip for a while. Now then, you just take it nice and easy, the doctor will be over later in the morning to talk to you.' She wrote down a few things on a sheet on a clipboard, placed it at the bottom of my bed, smiled, and then disappeared.

I tried to lift my head up, but I just couldn't do it. It felt like a lead balloon with a steel band playing inside it. So, I just closed my eyes, and surprisingly, despite the headache, I fell back to sleep easily enough.

'Hello there, Mrs Ali.'

I was awoken for the second time that morning by a voice I didn't recognise. I begrudgingly opened my eyes once more.

'I'm Dr Taylor. I'm a Consultant, and I am in charge of your care here today. You had quite a nasty fall young lady. Do you remember anything at all?'

The doctor was tall, and slim, and he had a strange moustache, sort of curled up at the edges. He had grey hair, and I think he wore grey clothes. Everything was sort of grey. And the red lips were next to him as well. He looked at me intently, obviously waiting for a response.

'Yes, I think so. I fell down the stairs.' My mind flicked back to the night before. I could picture Sohail and myself on the stairs. I was crying, pulling at his sleeve. I could see he pushed me away, and I began to fall. Then there was nothing. I couldn't see anything else. It was all blank after that.

'You did fall? I'm sorry to have to ask this, but we have to, you see. Your husband says you accidently fell down the stairs. Is that what happened? It was an accident?'

The doctor was focusing on my face. The nurse and her red lips were staring at me as well. I thought about it for a moment. He did push me away. On purpose or not, Sohail definitely pushed me, causing me to go hurtling down the stairs. But there were enough complications in my life at the moment. Did I really need any more? No, I had enough on my plate as it was.

'Yes, of course, it was an accident. It was just as my husband said.'

'Well, I bet you've got quite a sore head at the moment. That's the concussion. It should wear off after a couple of days, but in the meantime, you will get pain in your head and perhaps even nausea and dizziness. Don't worry yourself too much. It will pass; eventually.'

'When can I go home?' I don't know why on earth I asked. I didn't even want to go back to Sohail's house. But I didn't want to stay in a hospital either. I wanted to go back home, to my mum and dad's house. I wanted my mum. I just wanted my mum.

'You might be able to go home tomorrow. Maybe, we'll see. There is one other thing, though, that I must talk to you about.' The doctor's tone had now changed, he cleared his throat and he hesitated for a short time before he continued, which only served to increase my sense of nervousness about what he was going to say. 'Due to the fall, you suffered what we call a late miscarriage. I'm really very sorry, but there was nothing we could do. You have lost the baby. We had to give you some blood, and also carry out a surgical procedure.'

'Oh? What do you mean?' I asked, not really taking it in just yet.

'Well, as I said, you miscarried due to the fall. We had to put you under general anaesthetic, then take you to theatre and remove all the pregnancy tissue from your uterus. Also, we had to insert a tube down your throat to help with your breathing. Your throat may well feel painful and sore for a while, and clearly it is hoarse at the moment, but it will improve over the next couple of days.'

I just stared into the space in front of me. I couldn't quite comprehend it all. It took a little while for my hurting brain to process what I had just been told in a very matter of fact, albeit professional, way. The baby was gone? The baby was gone! Gone. And now I was all alone. Alone. Again.

'I know it's a lot to take in,' said the doctor, as he observed the blank yet shocked expression on my face, 'but there are people who can help you to come to terms with your sad loss, and nurse here will be only too happy to get you in touch with a counsellor if you want to talk things through. It really does help sometimes. So please, do let us know if you need any help to get you through this difficult time. There is a lot of excellent support and advice available should you wish to access it.'

As he spoke, I lay there motionless. I wasn't crying, I couldn't even speak. I was still and silent, staring straight ahead, into nothing. Sensing I was no longer listening, perhaps thinking they should probably just leave me to it, the grey figure and the red lips quietly disappeared. I didn't even see them go. I didn't even care. Not about them, or me, or anyone much. So I shut my eyes tight and hoped I could sleep. I wanted darkness and blackness. I didn't want to see. Or feel. Or hear.

Chapter 16: His verdict

JUST AS ON THE DAY we went home from the hospital after the scan, in silence, so too today we went home without either of us saying a word. There was just the opening and banging shut of the car doors, the clink-clunk of the seat belts, and the hushed growl of the engine.

As soon as I got into the house, I went straight to the lounge at the back. I wanted to look out into the garden, so I sat in my favourite chair by the window. I always enjoyed the view from this spot. It was serene, and comforting to the eye, and I knew it would give a moment or two's peace to my aching mind. I spied beautiful white anemones on the side closest to me, pretty, purple asters not far from the fountain, bright blue geraniums, Chinese lanterns and the most beautiful pink, peach, and yellow roses in the borders. And crimson roses. There were crimson roses too, but I always averted my gaze. Crimson still hurt my eyes, almost blindingly so.

Sohail had quietly dragged himself into the lounge behind me, and now went and sat opposite me. He gave out a little cough before he began to speak.

'I'm sorry for what happened to you. I only meant to push you off me, you wouldn't let go of me. You kept pulling at me, I mean, you were hysterical; do you remember? I really didn't mean for you to fall down the stairs.'

I continued to look out of the window in silence as he spoke. The sun was out, and the garden looked spectacular today. Perhaps I could plant some tulips when I felt better. I like tulips, I thought to myself. I would like pink and purple tulips. But I also liked marigolds. In fact, I loved marigolds; magnificently bright, vividly orange marigolds. As well as growing them in the back yard, my mum had planted some at my dad's grave. I didn't get to go to his grave very often. The last time I went was a week before the wedding. His grave was in a cemetery that was miles away from my mum's house. He had to be buried there because it had a Muslim section. Marigolds used to be his favourite flowers, and now they're my favourites too. In its own way, the humble marigold is a proud, majestic sort of a flower. Nothing to rival the sunflower in sheer height and size, but an equal or perhaps its superior in looks, I always thought.

'Selina, are you listening?' Sohail asked as he leaned over to try and get my attention. I turned to face him, but I may as well not have bothered. It's as if I saw straight through him. I just couldn't focus on his face.

'Like I said, I'm sorry about what happened, but it still doesn't take away the fact that you lied to me. You tried to trick me into bringing up someone else's kid. I can't forgive you for that. It was a horrendous thing to do.'

I began to focus now, and looked at him with a little more intent; his eyebrows were furrowed, and he had a grimace on his face. His nostrils were flaring slightly, and he breathed a little heavily, as though he was still enraged but was trying to tone it down. He sat with a slight bend forward, with his fists clenched. He had clearly formed his opinions; he had made his judgements based on his own presumptions.

'Am I not even going to be given a chance to explain?' I asked him.

'Explain? What is there to explain? The facts speak for themselves, surely. There's nothing you could say that could ever justify what you did. What explanation could you give me that would possibly make a difference? Did you give even an ounce of thought to my reputation, and my family's honour, and to what people would have said if this had got out? What on earth could you tell me now that would make any of this okay, or make it any less shameful or embarrassing,' he said, as he looked away in disgust. He couldn't even bear to look at me, I thought. He was that sickened by me and my evil deception, as he perceived it. I could feel a warm rage creeping up my neck and resting in my cheeks; he carried on with his stinging, self-righteous deluge.

'Do you honestly expect me to sit here and allow you to try and defend yourself? What lame excuse could you possibly come up with for such an appalling act? You have humiliated me, and by implication my family, to such a degree that no sob story is ever going to wash.'

'So, let me get this straight. You are certain that there is nothing I could say that would make you think differently of me. I mean, there can be absolutely nothing that, in your eyes, could ever vindicate me, and the decision I took, even slightly?'

Without any hesitation, he replied, 'No.'

I swallowed hard, sure in my mind that this one word had now determined my fate. I was clear in my mind as to what I had to do. 'If that is your decision; then fine. As soon as I'm physically able to do it, which I should think would be in a day or two's time, and in any event before your parents get back, I will pack my things and leave. It's obvious there is nothing here for me to stay for. But as a last request, I need to beg one favour of you.'

'What is it?' He was still looking away as he asked the question.

'Please, please, can you not tell your parents the real reason why I'm going? Don't tell them about the baby not being yours. Tell them anything else you want; I was a bad wife, I neglected you, the miscarriage was too much, it was my fault, anything, but not that. My mum is going to take the fact that we're separating badly enough, I don't think she will be able to handle the truth. Whatever you think of me, my mum knows nothing about what happened, and doesn't deserve to be hurt any more than she needs to be.'

Unlike the last answer which he had given like a bullet fired to kill, this time he hesitated for a few moments.

'It's fine,' he finally replied, sheepishly, 'I won't say anything. It would be embarrassing for me, too, to have to tell my parents the shameful truth. I don't want them to be dragged through the mud with such scandalous talk that would inevitably result if the truth were to come out. It's best if we just bury this here and now. I'd sooner just forget about it all. And to be frank, I'd sooner forget about you.'

Chapter 17: The journey back

THE TRAIN JOURNEY up to Leeds gave me plenty of time for some inner contemplation. The world now seemed to me to be a very harsh place indeed. My life had taken the most demented twists, and haphazard turns, that I could barely recognise any of my life before that hateful evening in June. I didn't want to believe it, but my instinct warned me that I was forever going to be consumed by the turmoil that evening had left in its wake. I wondered if I was ever going to be free of the shackles of that episode, which seemed to follow me like a grave shadow.

I looked out of the window, only to see the rain start to come down, when it had been sunny just a few minutes before. Sparkly, baby rain droplets gently fell upon the window, as the sky hurried in its pursuit to change from a hazy blue to a steely grey. After only a few minutes, there were large, angry raindrops mercilessly banging against the window. How quickly a soft, delicate, sunny outlook could transform into a heavy, rough, miserable riot, I thought to myself. I looked at my reflection in the window. How did I end up here? I went from being a happy, naive schoolgirl to a woman who had lost so much in what seemed like the blink of an eye.

I peered over to see an elderly couple opposite me, seated at a table, chatting away. The man had a definite grandad look about him; he was wearing a checked, flat-cap, a blue anorak, dark green corduroys and hush puppies. And spectacles on the end of his nose, which he obviously needed to do his crossword. The lady seemed a little younger, and was quite glamorous, with her bright, coral lipstick and immaculately manicured nails. She pulled out a sandwich box and a flask of what seemed like tea. As they ate and drank, laughed and joked. I wondered what people like these two worried about. Did they have anything to worry about? They just looked happy, and in love, whatever either of those was.

I got off the connecting train at Bradford station and caught a taxi to my mum's house. I hadn't given any word to my mother that I was coming. I didn't want to face a barrage of questions before I got there. I hadn't even told my mum about the miscarriage, yet.

I looked out of the window for the duration of the fifteen-minute drive as I sat in the back of the taxi. As the car approached our neighbourhood, I saw all the familiar sights that I had grown up with; my old school playing fields, where I had been whacked around the ankles in the freezing cold when we played hockey in the icy winter, and the locally famous "black hill" at the bottom end of the school fields, which we used to race to the top of, still sitting in its dark, shadowy glory. There was the parade of shops on the high street, selling everything from fish and chips to household bargains to Asian sweets and savouries. I knew every little corner of this area. It was no Four Oaks with its million-pound-plus, individually crafted properties that had small parks for their back gardens, and driveways the length of half a street. But it was home. It was all I had known as home. The taxi drove past the road, which led to the Qureshis' house, and I drew back away from the window. I wasn't sure how I was going to face the dreaded inevitability of having to see him. But I flung those thoughts out of my head a couple of minutes later when the taxi pulled up outside my old home—my real home. Nothing much had changed since I had left, the house and the rest of the street looked exactly the same. But I feared that I had changed so much, yet again.

My mum opened the door and was shocked to see me, but in a good sort of a way, as she assumed that her happily married daughter and beloved son-in-law were paying her a surprise visit. She hugged and kissed me, and hurried me into the hallway.

'Selina! Come in out of the rain, come on. Where is Sohail? Has he gone to park the car? It's always such a problem parking on our street, and I worry about his expensive car. What if someone scratches it, or worse still, steals it. That would be terrible. Why didn't you say you were coming? I would have made some nice food. I would have cooked all your favourites. But no matter, it is early yet, I have plenty of time to cook.'

As I walked through she noticed I had a large suitcase, but didn't make any comment. She left the door ajar expecting Sohail would follow shortly.

'Mum, close the door, please. Sohail isn't with me,' I said to her.

'Oh, I just thought. Well, never mind, I suppose he couldn't come because of work. Come on then, I will go and put the kettle on, and get you a nice cup of tea. I've got some of those lemon puff biscuits you like so much; they've always been your favourites, haven't they? You know, even though you don't live here anymore, I keep buying all the things you like. Lemon puffs, salt and vinegar crisps, pomegranates, HP sauce. You know only you used to eat all these things. Me and Adam never touch them, apart from the pomegranates. I do enjoy those myself. And you know your brother prefers cheese and onion. Anyway, I will go get the biscuits and the tea.'

'Please mum, just forget the tea, and come and sit down,' I said as I walked into the living room. My mum followed straight after me. 'Is Adam at school?' I asked her. He probably was, but I thought I should check, just in case.

'Yes, he is. Selina, what's the matter?' The angst was showing on her face as she asked the question. She was now clearly worried.

I sat down on our old, reassuringly comfy sofa next to her, and held her hand.

'Mum, I've got some bad news. I'm sorry, I know how much you were looking forward to it, but, I've lost the baby.'

My mum stared at me with a look of devastation on her face. She had really not anticipated this at all. I had to brace myself, as this was only round one of the disappointments, and the bigger bombshell was yet to come.

'Oh my goodness! You poor thing! When did this happen? And why didn't you call me? You should have let me know, I would have come down, or at least phoned you. What must your husband and his family have thought, that I didn't help you at all.'

'It was just a few days ago, and I didn't tell you because there was nothing you could have done.'

'What happened? How did it happen?' My mum was going to insist on knowing every detail.

'It was just an accident mum, I fell down the stairs, and they couldn't do anything to save the baby. The baby's gone, and I'm coming to terms with it.'

'I'm so sorry *beti*, I don't know what else to say,' she said as she consoled me, with tears in her own eyes. I'm not sure who needed consoling more.

'But that's not all mum. There's something else I need to tell you.' I pressed her hand a little harder, maybe to steady myself, more than to prepare her for round two. 'It's about me and Sohail. Now please keep calm when I tell you. The thing is; we've split up.'

Her jaw dropped, and she just stared at me for a few moments, open-mouthed, unable to quite take in the blow that I had just dealt her.

Here it comes, I thought. The tirade will begin any second now...

'Split up! What do you mean "split up"? How ridiculous. I never heard such a thing. Nobody splits up after just a couple of months of marriage. You've been married all of two days, and you've "split up". And that too, after you have just had a miscarriage! I don't understand what's going on here. This is unbelievable. Perhaps you'd better explain young lady. And I want to hear everything.'

'There's nothing to explain mum. Please, don't stress yourself out. There's no big dramatic story to tell. We simply weren't getting along, in fact we never actually got along from the start, and things didn't really improve. And after the miscarriage, well, that was it, really. There was nothing keeping us together after that. We're not right for each other, and we don't make each other happy. I don't think I'm what he was looking for. And he's not really the one for me either. I'm sorry mum, we tried, but it just didn't work out.'

My mum's face was red with rage. The second piece of bad news had really done it. I think she could just about cope with the miscarriage, because in her eyes that was God's will, but the news of the separation hadn't gone down at all well, much as I had expected. This was not God's will. In my mum's way of thinking, this was salvageable—she probably fully believed that Sohail and I were being silly about "not getting on" and that we would be able to sort it out, and if not, she would try and sort it out for us. She was not going to take this lying down. In her mind, you worked at a marriage no matter what the obstacles or issues life threw in your way, as marriage was a life-long commitment, not like a handbag you buy from a shop but return the following week because you didn't like it after all.

'I'm not having this,' she shouted. 'He can't just send you away like this on your own, so soon after you lost your baby. It's not acceptable. And what about his parents, what do they have to say about this, huh? This is an outrage. Pass me the phone, I'm going to phone him and find out what's going on here. If he thinks I'm just going to take this, let him get away with treating you in this way, then he's got another thing coming. This has to be sorted out. I won't allow this to happen to you. I will speak to him, make him see sense, and then I am sure he will come round.'

'No mum! There's no point in you speaking to him. I told you, it's over!'

'Well then, I will have to talk to his parents; let's see what they make of it all!'

'You can't speak to them right now, they're on holiday. They're not back until tomorrow. Please mum, just drop it. It's done with.'

'Okay then, I will phone them tomorrow. I'm not leaving it like this Selina, you are my daughter. How can I just let it go? He has more or less thrown you out just a few days after your miscarriage, and you expect me to keep quiet?'

There was no arguing with my mum right then. And I was absolutely exhausted. So I let my mum carry on having her say for a while longer, until she felt satisfied that by ranting and raving for as long as she was permitted to, without objection or interruption, she had at least done something about what she perceived to be a gross injustice. Once I was content that she had let off enough steam, I excused myself. All I wanted to do right then was to go to sleep; back in my own bed.

Chapter 18: A sigh of relief

'I SEE. YES. Well, when you put it like that. I suppose so. Although I have to say, he shouldn't have let her come like that so soon after her miscarriage, however much she was insisting on it. If Sohail really couldn't stop her, then he should have at least driven her up.... Well, no one is more sorry than me. It is such a shame. I never thought it would end like this. But she is my daughter, and you know what our people can be like. I'm never going to stop tongues wagging, am I? No matter what, they will always blame the girl. It's never the boy's fault, is it? They will always lay the burden of fault with the girl. But if it is their *kismet*, if this is their destiny, then there is nothing you or I can do. It seems as though they have both made up their minds. And I guess we have to accept it.'

My mum put the telephone down and came and sat by me on the sofa in the living room where I had taken root of late. I was flicking through the channels, trying to find any programme on daytime TV of the slightest bit of interest. It was a toss-up between a programme about searching for long-lost heirs to small fortunes, or the rival channel with a show about decorating the house of some poor victim who was going to come back home and see that her previously quite stylish bedroom now looked like some old French boudoir.

My mum was clearly saddened by what she had been told on the telephone, so I switched the telly off.

'I did tell you mum.' I said to her as she came and sat by me, looking dejected.

'Yes,' she cried, 'you did tell me, and so did your aunty Ruby just now. That it is over. And they are accepting it and moving on, and I should do the same.'

My mum looked so disappointed, like a big heavy weight
was back on her shoulders again. It was that big burden she
had talked about, I thought. And seeing her like this in turn
made me feel despondent, so much so that I couldn't even
think of anything to say, to even try and say, to make my mum
feel better. So I didn't.

Over dinner that evening, Adam and mum filled me in on
the events since I had been away, whilst we tucked into my
mum's famously delicious spicy *karahi* lamb and homemade
naans. Mercifully, I was back to eating meat and spices again. I
sure had missed my mum's food. It was homely and
comforting, and gave me a warm, fuzzy feeling nothing else
could quite replicate.

They told me that sadly, Barbara from down the road had
died a few weeks ago. She was eighty-seven years old. Poor
Brian was all alone now. My siblings and I had always had a
soft spot for the lovely Brian and Barbara, who had always
given us stockings full of sweets and chocolates every
Christmas for as long as we could remember, and not
forgetting all the Easter eggs, and goodies on our birthdays.
And we had always taken them *mitai* and *samosas* every Eid, and
presents at Christmas. They were a childless couple now.
They'd had one daughter, Margaret, but tragically, she had
passed away many years ago when she was only seventeen, on
New Year's Eve. The sadness had never left them. They had a
black-and-white photograph of her on the old mantelpiece. I
often used to gaze at it, as I thought Margaret was so beautiful,
like one of those film stars from the black-and-white movies.
She had a look of Ingrid Bergman about her, her silky soft,
pin-curled hair parted gently at the side, her dewy eyes looking
straight at you. It made me feel sad, even as a young child,
every time I looked at it.

'But the neighbours have all been looking in on him. So
I'm sure he will be okay, although no doubt after so many
years of marriage, he will miss her terribly,' mum continued.

'The Karim family had a wedding a few weeks ago, their eldest son got married, at long last. I mean he must be at least thirty now. The bride is very educated you know; she is a pharmacist. She works in that big chemist on Market Street I believe. She looked very beautiful in her red gold and cream coloured *lengha*, I have to say. And she had very nice jewellery; she had it specially made in Pakistan to match her outfit, which was also stitched over there, in Lahore. Of course Lahore is very famous for its shopping and fashion houses. There is so much choice; Anarkali, Liberty Market, Mall Road, the Fort. And all the big designers work from there too. I was only fortunate to go to Lahore once, with a school trip, but it was wonderful. I was so mesmerised.' My mum was looking upward, as though she was actually back there as she spoke. 'The Shahi Fort was standing majestically overlooking the old city, and the Shalimar Gardens were a true testament to the Mughal architecture; three symmetrical terraces of gardens, dotted with hundreds of fountains, and all kinds of trees. And how could I forget, the grand Badshahi Mosque sat right next to the Fort. It was built by Emperor Aurangzeb, you know. And it is absolutely huge; you cannot imagine the space in that mosque. I really do have to take you two there sometime. It's a shame we never had the time when I took you to Pakistan when you were younger. But the security situation was not good even then. I do despair for my country sometimes.'

My mother continued, with a sigh, partly for the sorry state of Pakistan at the moment, but mainly to reminisce about her youthful trip of bygone years, until she remembered something of present relevance. 'Oh, and another bit of news, I almost forgot, your uncle Zubair has gone to work abroad until next year.'

I hadn't really been listening properly to what my mum had been saying so far, but this really grabbed my attention, for I had been absolutely dreading the mention of his name, let alone the prospect of seeing him.

'Really? How come?' I tried to sound as casual as possible.

'He had a great opportunity come his way to spend a year in the UAE heading up some new university department, so he is going to be there until next summer. He is in Sharjah I think, or was it Abu Dhabi? Anyway, it's somewhere around there, and they're paying him a lot of money for it, and his living expenses too. Their eldest son is back from University now having finished his degree, so at least Sajda is not alone in the house. He is working as a Trainee Manager at some bank or other; I can't remember where she said.'

Deep down, somewhere inside me in the very pit of my stomach, I breathed the most enormous sigh of relief. In my quest to get away from my attacker, I hadn't made any headway at all, as I was back where I had begun, just a stone's throw away from where it had all happened. And the fear of seeing him again had made my head ache and body shiver. But this was the best news that I could ever have possibly heard. I could now just get on with my life without fear of bumping into him, at least not for a while. It felt like the first bit of freedom I had experienced since the night of June 14th. Life could now begin again. But before that, I had to deal with the fall out of my return.

Chapter 19: Interfering busy bodies

I WAS FINISHING getting ready upstairs, tying my long, black hair into a ponytail, when I heard the old man's voice as he entered the house, and then his wife's mutterings straight after him.

'We heard about the very sad news of your daughter being sent back home by her husband, and thought we would come and see how you are, Sister, and if there was anything we could do to help.'

Help yourself to your pound of gossip, I thought, as I came down and listened in from the hallway when they had gone into the lounge. And stick your oar in where it's not wanted, I muttered to myself.

Haji Sultan was about seventy years old, and he was a relative on my dad's side. He had a long, silver beard, was slightly chubby and had a perfectly round face. He always wore his white mosque hat and had little round, brown, framed glasses that dropped too far down his nose. He used a walking stick, claiming he had a dodgy knee, but I'm sure that was just for effect. His wife was tall and skinny, with a pointy face, and a hairy mole on her chin. As a child, I had always thought that she looked like the witch from the 'Wizard of Oz', and he like the wizard. She looked every bit as evil and he was not at all wise.

'Thank you for coming, it is very kind of you to look in on me. No, there is nothing you can do, I'm afraid, Brother, they have sent her home for good it seems and there is not much chance of them taking her back,' said mum in her saddest voice.

'But what happened, Rashida,' asked Mrs Sultan. On hearing her squawky voice, I suddenly remembered how, as kids, we all used to run upstairs and sing the song "Ding Dong the Wicked Witch is Dead" after she used to leave. Once my mum had heard us, and we got a right royal telling off for being disrespectful.

'I mean, it is not like them to behave in this way, from what I know of them,' the Wicked Witch continued. 'And really, there is no smoke without fire is there? Something must have happened for them to do this.'

'What do you mean?' my mum immediately snapped back. She was clearly not happy with that last comment and the connotations it threw our way.

'What my wife means is that it is not right what has happened,' intervened her husband, sensing his wife's comment may have irritated my mum a little, 'and if you want, I can telephone them and have a word with them. I can try and make them see sense, and take your girl back. You know, we are family, and we only have your best interests at heart. We know how difficult it must be for you, a woman all alone, a widow at your time of life, having to deal with so much sadness and heartache. You won't be able to stop the gossips Rashida. They will talk openly and will try and suggest that Selina is to blame. You know they will say she must have done something wrong. It is better for you if she goes back. This is best for your *izzat*. So, do you want me to have a word?'

More like do some digging and find out what really happened. Time to put an end to this nonsense, I thought.

'No we don't!' I said, as I swept into the room suddenly and took them all by surprise.

'Selina!' said my mother, but what the expression on her face was saying was, "Don't be so rude".

'What I mean, Uncle *ji*, is thank you so much for your concern, and it's not that we don't appreciate it. We do, of course we do, but I think it's best if you stay out of it. And I'm thinking about your *izzat* when I say this. Suppose you ring them, and they are rude to you, and they do your *besti*, then we will feel bad that such a well-respected leader of the community, a highly regarded elder of the *bradri* such as yourself, has been humiliated because of us, because of me. I think that would be a terrible thing, and that would be *besti* for *us*. I simply could not bear that.'

'Well, if you put it like that,' replied Uncle Sultan, and the Wicked Witch nodded reluctantly, in a disgruntled manner.

'Selina, go and make the tea,' said mum, glad that the conversation was over.

'Yes mum, I will, only I think I saw a delivery van pulling up outside Uncle's house just a few seconds ago with a parcel maybe—'

'Really? Oh no, quick we must rush,' said the old man, and with that they both disappeared hurriedly out of the house, the old man suddenly finding his knee working splendidly well without the walking stick after all.

'Selina was there any need for that?' asked my mum.

'Frankly, *amee ji*, yes, there was. I am sick of these so-called relatives cum community elders and leaders sticking their noses in where they're not wanted. From now on, mum, please try and have less to do with these people. They're just do-gooders who never actually do anything good for anyone. They're self-obsessed, condescending, smug hypocrites. And you know all those traits are anti-Islamic before you say I'm being rude or acting against our religious beliefs.'

'Selina, what's happened to you? You know full well that all these people have been very good to me, to us, in these last couple of very difficult years. Yes, some of them can be a bit gossipy, I am well aware of that, but at the same time they have helped me enormously. They have been very kind.'

'Not all of them mum.'

'Anyway, where are you going all dressed up?' mum asked me, noticing my smart blue suit and black document wallet.

'I'm going to go and hand out my CV to a few places. Now that I'm back and not studying, I really do need to get a job.'

I spent the next couple of months scouring the newspaper ads and various websites, applying for any suitable jobs. I managed to get a few interviews. One at the local supermarket to stack shelves, one at an accountants' office for the post of a receptionist, and one at a busy city centre firm of solicitors as a legal assistant.

On the 18th December, I turned nineteen, but I was determined not to celebrate. In view of everything that had happened to me in the previous year, the last thing I wanted was a party or any kind of a fuss. I just wanted a quiet day, without any ceremony. So we kept it simple. Adam went and got some fish and chips from a new take away that had opened recently on the high street, which had received the thumbs up from most of the neighbours, and being a teenage boy who was always hungry and thinking about food, this was not too arduous a task for him. My mum baked me a little cake; it was round, covered with pink buttercream icing, and decorated with dark- and white-chocolate love-hearts and edible, pink flowers. So we "celebrated" with a nice, quiet meal, and later, I watched Sandra Bullock's "While You Were Sleeping" to send me off to bed with a warm, cosy feeling. As my head hit the pillow, I shut my eyes and I thought, just for a second, about how wonderful it would be to experience true, good, old-fashioned romance; for a man to love me like the heroes loved the girls in the movies. To know what warm, tender, heart-warming love was. The nineties chick flicks always seemed to be the best for the most perfect, sweetest endings. Somehow, after everything that had happened to me, I feared this would remain an unobtainable fantasy for me. Love and romance seemed so appealing in the movies, but that was where they would remain. I couldn't see myself becoming close to any man after the male misery in my life so far.

On the very next day, unlike on my birthday, I was much more in the mood to celebrate. I came running and screaming down the stairs to my mum in the kitchen and gave her a great big hug.

'What's all this about?' mum asked, as the egg she was holding dropped out of her hands and cracked on the floor. I nearly knocked her over too, just as she was about to start frying the eggs for breakfast.

'What is it you *jinn*? What's all this noise in aid of?' She always referred to me as a *jinn* when she thought I was behaving in a daft, unladylike manner.

'Mum, I got it! I got the job! I just got an email now saying so!'

'Speak slowly Selina! Which job did you get?'

'The one at the law firm! I got the job as a legal assistant. Oh my God, I'm so excited. It's only a temporary contract for six months, to cover maternity leave, but I can't wait. I'll be working there until the end of June next year, and you never know, they might keep me on for longer. It's in the criminal department, and I just know I'm going to love it!'

'That's fantastic news Selina. I really am pleased for you, and proud of you, my darling. When do you start?' she said, whilst upside-down, cleaning up the egg.

'On the 5th of January! I just cannot wait!'

'*Shabash*! Well done. Now come, eat some breakfast, it's eggs, toast and beans. Well, it will be if you let me finish making it, that is,' said mum, smiling as she cracked a fresh egg into the pan.

Chapter 20: Off to work I go

FINALLY, THE 5TH OF JANUARY ARRIVED, and I made sure I turned up to work on my first day in good time.

'Take a seat,' the receptionist said. She was a very cheerful, quite elderly lady, with short curly grey hair and small frameless spectacles. She had a large, extremely chunky necklace and bracelet on, which clinked and clanked as she took calls and wrote down messages. I sat quietly in the reception of Connors Solicitors, as she slurped her coffee rather loudly, which I couldn't help but be irritated by.

Another lady came into the reception area and held out her hand to shake mine. She was in her late twenties, or maybe early thirties. She had long, immaculately straight, blond hair—she was clearly very good with the old straighteners. She was tall, and a little plump. She was well dressed, and wore a black, mid-length skirt and a purple chiffon blouse, with a beaded sparkly purple bracelet to match. Her smart, black kitten-heeled shoes finished the look.

'Selina? I'm Rachel, very pleased to meet you.'

'Pleased to meet you, too,' I replied, as I shook her hand.

'Well, Selina, come on through and I will introduce you to everyone and show you to your desk.'

I followed right behind her, through a long, wide corridor, and into a room right at the end on the left-hand side. It was quite large with about seven desks, and a large photocopier to one side. The offices were all over-flowing with files, and trays, and papers, everywhere. As the filing cabinets were jam packed, the piles just grew on the top, on the floor, on the desks, all over the place really.

Rachel introduced me to the other women in the room, for they were all women. Rachel worked in the criminal department, which is where I would be assisting her. In addition, there were Susan and Diane in Civil Litigation, Roshni and Margaret in Family and Probate, and June and Heather in Property.

She then showed me to my desk at the far end by the window, facing inward toward the door. After showing me what was what on the computer system, using the telephones, the fax machine and sharing the general administrative information, she introduced me to the cashier, Jenny. Then we went off so she could show me some other areas of the building that were of note; the stationary cupboard, the kitchen for the teas and coffees, and, of course, the ladies room. The offices were all decorated in fairly neutral tones, with beige walls, white skirting boards, brown wooden doors, and modern lighting. There were some framed pictures along the corridor, but this was the only area in the whole place that was not cluttered.

We were passing the room of the Senior Criminal Solicitor, Mr Connor, who was also the founder of the firm, and we were going to pop in to say hello, but as it turned out, he wasn't in, so then Rachel knocked on the office of Mr Dean instead.

'This is Mo's office.' Rachel informed me.

'Come in,' came a voice from the other side of the door. Mo wore a crisply tailored, black suit. His dark brown hair was smartly trimmed and parted to the side. His emerald-green eyes looked striking as they stared out from a pale-coloured face, and he exuded an air of confidence and gravitas beyond his obviously youthful age.

'I know you're probably just about to leave for the morning court session, but I thought I would introduce you to our new recruit, Selina. She's here for the six months' cover.'

'Good morning Selina,' Mo said, reaching over to shake my hand. 'It's great to meet you. I hope Rachel isn't going to work you too hard on your first day,' he said.

I just smiled back.

'Don't be silly. I only do that once they get to like me, and then they can't say no!' Rachel laughed.

'Well, I've got to get to Court. I'm running late as ever, so I will see you later, perhaps,' he said, looking down for the most part, as he crammed some files and loose papers into his briefcase.

'Yes, see you.' I said, finally finding my voice.

I went back to my desk and continued to receive my induction for the day from Rachel. There was a lot to cover; how they dealt with enquiries, issues of confidentiality, the need to make impeccable file notes, and practical things like the fire escape and which sandwich shop was the best one to go to, although the girls were divided on that. I was nervous when I had first arrived, but told myself by the middle of the day that I needn't have been, as I was taking to it already.

Within a week of working at Connors I was told very encouragingly that I had settled into my job extremely well. I actually got on with Rachel as though we had been great friends for the longest time. She had an easy, comfortable nature about her, and that meant I could go to her whenever I needed to, which was quite often at first, and mercifully she was always happy to help with anything I didn't understand.

It was the beginning of week two, and I had just got in and went off to make some tea for myself and Rachel whilst she took a call.

When I walked back in with the mugs of tea, I heard Rachel say, 'That's okay, I will let Mohammed know you called, thank you again.' She finished a phone call.

'Who is Mohammed?' I asked, as I handed her tea to her. I hadn't heard that name here before, at least not in the criminal department.

'Oh, that's Mo, his full name is Mohammed Dean, but we call him Mo for short because it's easier. What did you think it stood for?'

'I don't know; I wasn't sure really. I have heard Mohammed shortened to Mo before, of course, but I didn't think he looked like a Mohammed.'

'No,' she said, 'it's definitely Mohammed. You sound surprised.'

'Yes, well, I didn't realise, I mean, he looks—'

'Very English, and not a bit Pakistani? Well, he is, in a manner of speaking, half of him anyway. You see, his dad is Pakistani, and his mum is English, a Yorkshire woman born and bred. So as a family, they have both cultures, Eid and Christmas! I have to say his mum has over the years adopted aspects of the Pakistani lifestyle as though she was born into it. She makes the most lip-smackingly good *samosas* and *pakoras* for the staff parties! And she looks very graceful in her *salwar kameez* suits. They are a lovely family, actually.'

This did surprise me, as he had looked and talked like an Englishman, through and through. He just did. His dual heritage came as a surprise. I wasn't sure at times what I actually was, especially when I was younger, as it was sometimes really tricky trying to reconcile my different backgrounds. What *was* my identity? This was a question I had pondered over many a time. It had perplexed me awfully when I was around twelve, thirteen years old. I was born in Great Britain, so I was British, definitely. I did feel that now. I was a British person with Pakistani heritage. So I was a British Pakistani. And I was a Muslim too. So I was a British Pakistani Muslim. But was I *English*? I instinctively knew the answer to this one. I never saw myself as English. The Queen was English. Benedict Cumberbatch was English. No, I thought, I was not English. Nor was I ever likely to be. But being British was enough for me.

'Selina, I need you to come to court with me,' yelled Mo from his office, which was exactly opposite mine, and in fact, if both doors were open we had a good view of each other. I could see him shuffling through some papers on his desk whilst he shouted across toward me.

'Oh, okay,' I said in reply, turning to Rachel for guidance as I stopped by her desk on my way out. 'Why do I need to go to court?' I asked her nervously.

She stopped what she was doing and turned to explain. 'You will be doing this kind of thing regularly, but it's nothing to worry about. Just go along and follow orders. For the most part you will have to take notes in court, but it's easy enough, as long as you can write really fast. You may have to develop your own unique abbreviations to keep up! And to be honest a lot of the time it is likely that you will have to do a bit of dogsbody work, running around here and there, sometimes a bit of meet and greet, or delivering messages. Just grab a notepad and pen, and follow Mo. He will tell you exactly what to do. And take your coat.'

I walked off, feeling slightly nervous. Ten minutes later we arrived on foot at the Crown Court. Mo quickly scanned the notice board in the foyer.

'Right, it's Court 2, come one,' said Mo, as he darted up the stairs with his long legs striding up two steps at a time, and I followed in haste behind him, finding it hard to keep up as he ran a hundred miles an hour.

'Okay, here is the courtroom, just through those doors.' said Mo as we reached the top. 'It's a robbery case. I need to go down to the cells to see the client. You wait here for the barrister. He's called David Evans. Go into the court and wait on our side of the benches at the front, and tell him I've gone down to see our man and will fill him in when I get back. Tell him that in the meantime, he needs to speak to the Prosecution Barrister as they're saying they've got some new evidence they want to put before the court.'

'Okay,' I replied with a bit of a squeak in my voice.

'Have you got all of that? Are you sure?' There was a mist of doubt in his eyes.

'Yes of course, that's fine,' I said, trying to convey an air of confidence, but really not at all sure of what I was doing.

I held my note pad tight against my chest, and went into the courtroom, but there was no one there as yet. I looked around and noticed that the courtroom itself was large and imposing, and had a feel of drama about it, like it had seen countless unexpected tales unfold before a startled jury amidst gasps from the public gallery and demands for "order" from the Judge. It was truly a stage set for drama and mystery, twists and turns. It was old-fashioned, still stuck in the shades of a distant past. The seating and desks were antique originals, crafted from dark wood to give a sense of sombreness. The Judge's area was raised, as you would expect, but the public gallery was raised far higher, for maximum theatrical effect.

I hovered near the seats and desks toward the front for a minute or two. Then a fully-wigged-and-robed barrister walked in, and he was whistling as he did so.

He stopped whistling and glanced in my direction. 'Hello,' he said to me with a smile

'Hello, are you, Mr Evans?'

'No, I'm not. I'm the Prosecutor, Andrew Leyland. I haven't seen you around here before. I'm sure I would have remembered a beautiful face like yours.'

I blushed a little, and luckily for me someone else walked in, and it looked like yet another barrister.

'Ah, this is your man, he said, as he turned to look at Mr Evans. 'David, this pretty little thing was asking for you. What does a nice young lady want with an old fogey like you, eh?'

'Hey, less of the old,' retorted David, 'and less of the fogey. You can speak for yourself!'

'I'm Selina, I just started at Connors Solicitors. Mo asked me to find you. He said to tell you that he's gone down to see the client and that the other Barrister wants to present some new evidence or something,' and I looked at Andrew Leyland as I finished the sentence. Mr Leyland had a wry smile on his face.

'Oh, he does now, does he?' was his response, staring at the Prosecutor as well.

The two men then started exchanging technical phrases about section number so and so, and such and such an Act. I sighed ever so slightly, as I realised that I had such a lot to learn, and there was so much I wanted to know. Soon, the court started filling up, and the defence barrister, clocking on to the fact that I was a complete novice, kindly motioned to me as to where I should sit to take notes. A couple of minutes later, Mo came and sat next to me. The Judge then entered the courtroom. Everyone stood up and then sat back down. Each barrister spoke a few words. The Judge then spoke briefly, after which everyone stood up once again and the Judge made a sharp exit.

Mo started walking out, and I followed in pursuit. I seemed to be doing a lot of that today.

'What's happening?' I asked, trying to keep up with him, again.

'There's going to be an adjournment whilst the Judge considers the Prosecution's application to introduce new evidence. I'm starving, let's go have some breakfast.'

'Okay. I'll follow you then, shall I?' I said with a note of sarcasm in my tone, but Mo was so hungry he didn't even notice. I continued, 'So, lead the way to the cafe, obviously I don't know my way around this place yet.'

'You'd better put your coat on; we're off to the Magistrates Court.'

'What? Why are we going all the way over there? Don't they have a cafe here?'

'Yes, of course, they do, but the Mags do proper toast.'

'What do you mean, "proper toast".'

'Betty does the softest toast, freshly buttered,' he said, all dreamy-eyed, looking up as though he was having a vision of it as he spoke. 'It's all golden and delicious, not like the cardboard they dish out here. Here, it's half-burnt to death, cold, and served with an even colder square of spread. Yuk! So come on, chop chop, we don't have long you know.'

We got caught in a generous sprinkling of rain as we dashed across, and I was so glad to be out of the rain, as we sat and devoured the admittedly totally delicious, golden toast with a hot mug of tea each. I thought Mo was so right; Betty's toast really was something to write home about. Betty herself was no less appealing than the toast, in a granny-like way, as she greeted each and every customer with the warmest smile, asked them how they were, told them how splendid it was to see them again, and so on.

As I was starting my second piece, a young man came up to Mo, who instantly got up, and then they high fived each other. The guy then turned to look at me.

'Is this your bird?' he asked Mo.

'I'm not a bird, his or anyone else's,' I cut in before Mo could answer.

'No, this is a new member of staff, Selina. And Selina, this is Craig, one of our clients.'

I really wasn't sure what to make of this Craig at all. He was quite tall, painfully skinny, with a shaved head and lots and lots of tattoos. In fact, I couldn't find any skin without a tattoo on it other than on his face; his arms hands and neck were plastered with skulls and bones and names. He had a rather intriguing nose ring. And a really, really strong Yorkshire accent.

'So, what are you doing here Craig, and more importantly, why don't I know about it. I hope you haven't got yourself another Solicitor.'

'No, no, I'm 'ere with a mate. For moral support like. I've been out for ten months now. Got a girlfriend and a baby on way 'n all. Got no plans to go inside no more. Defo on the straight 'n narrow now. Even got meeself a job. Just helping a brickie mate wi' all fetchin' an' carryin' but at least it pays the bills.'

'Good man! You keep it that way, do you hear.' They high fived again, and Craig walked off.

'Is he a regular client then?' I asked, wondering what sort of stuff Craig got up to that would land him in court.

'Yes, you could say that. I've represented him since he was about fourteen or fifteen, oh about five years now. He's not a bad lad at heart. Not really. People have this general image of all criminals being ruthless and cruel. But he's not an evil person, not at all, he's just a product of his background and the disadvantaged start he had in life. Some of these kids just don't stand a chance. He was in and out of care for all his young life. I remember when he used to be in the juvenile courts, he'd always look round to see if his mum had come. But she never did. I think all that boy ever craved was his mum's attention. But she was never there for him. His dad left when he was two or three and hasn't surfaced since. He was always either in a care home or prison. Not much difference between the two sometimes when you look at it. But I think if he is in a steady relationship and has a baby on the way, and is working, that could be all the incentive he needs to stay out of prison. But sometimes, you just see history repeating itself, and the child becomes the father, in and out of prison, and the cycle continues. But let's hope not, eh.'

In that moment, I had to acknowledge to myself what a lucky person I was. Despite my recent misfortunes, at least I knew the love of good parents. It's that unique, sweet love that no one else can give you. That no one else is capable of giving you. But this was tempered by a feeling of sadness in my heart, as I knew that I would have given that same love to my child had it survived.

Chapter 21: The kiss

I CONTINUED TO GROW in confidence in my work, and enjoyed it more and more as time went by. I had now been at Connors exactly three months, and I couldn't believe how far I had come. And neither could the others. I was like a sponge they told me, constantly taking it all in, learning all the time.

Mo and I continued to work closely together, and by now there was constant joking and leg-pulling as we walked and sometimes ran to the local courts, and drove around in his sporty, red BMW between the courts a bit further afield, stretching from Yorkshire to the other side of the Pennines. Mo never knew where he was going to be most days until he got in and saw who was locked up where, but with his trials he usually asked me to come and do my stuff. My hand would be about to drop off at the end of the day after all the note taking. But I enjoyed every minute of it. Sometimes we would do up to three courts in a day, and often they would be miles apart. And then there were the prison visits. They were a bit depressing. It was always sad to see a person, especially women who were often as young as me, confined in that way. You wondered how they ended up there in the first place, and what got them through the long days and nights spent behind bars.

It was a Friday evening, and as it was Mr Connor's birthday. They were all going out for drinks after work to celebrate before they headed home. Naturally, they asked me to come along too.

'But I don't drink,' I told Rachel, not sure in my own mind if I should go. I hadn't really been working there very long. I thought I was going to feel out of place.

'Well, neither does Mo, or a couple of the others, and they're all coming. Come on; just get an orange juice or something.'

'Okay, I'll just phone my mum and tell her I'll be a bit late.'

Ever since I had come back from Birmingham, my mum had become much more relaxed with me. I think a part of her felt guilty for pushing me into a marriage that I hadn't really wanted, so that she could cross out that box which had said "unmarried daughter at home" and tick the one that said "married daughter living happily with husband". When it had gone pear-shaped, I was surprised that she didn't blame me at all, and took it in her stride much more than I could have hoped. She blamed herself for cornering me into agreeing with her choice. She thought she had more or less forced me into the marriage, and now my future was ruined, and for that she was regretful. But in reality, I felt even more guilty that she should think this, for the decision to marry Sohail, in the end, had been entirely my own. And I couldn't even tell her.

Down at the pub, Mr Connor and a few of the others were very merry by seven o'clock, and definitely making the most of the occasion. The beers and gin and tonics kept coming, and the laughter kept getting louder and louder, and some of the jokes ruder and ruder. He gave a small speech, thanking all of his members of staff for their hard work and so on. I noticed the time on my watch and thought I ought to make a move. Mo overheard me telling Rachel, and offered to give me a lift.

'Are you sure? I don't want to put you out of your way.' I thought he lived in the other direction.

'Of course, it's not a problem,' he reassured me, and with that we said our good nights and left.

There was a bit of an awkward silence between us as we walked up the hill toward the car, which I couldn't really understand. Maybe he was tired, I thought. Or maybe it was nothing, and I was just imagining things.

When we got to the car, as I was about to open the door, Mo took my arm away from the door. I turned to look at him, wondering what was going on. He was looking straight at me, his eyebrows slightly frayed, then without saying another word, he moved closer to kiss me. This came as a complete shock to me. I was aghast at the sight of his head moving toward me, and his lips making their way to meet mine. Although his lips had barely brushed mine, I saw red, and quickly descended into a spinning rage. I pushed him away with both my hands, with full force, so violently in fact, that he stumbled and almost fell over. How did I not see it coming? Again! Why was this happening to me, yet again?

'Get away from me, don't touch me, do you hear, don't you dare touch me!' I screamed at the top of my voice, and then just ran off.

'Selina, wait!' he shouted after me.

He caught up with me and grabbed my arm, which I started to wrestle away.

'Okay, okay,' he said, holding his arms up in the air.

'I don't want a lift from you, do you hear? I don't want anything from you. I'll make my own way home!' I said, in floods of tears by this time. To say he looked shocked was an understatement. After all, I had just pretty much attacked him. I was physically shaking, and I looked away, not wanting to meet his gaze.

'Hey, hey, Selina please, I'm sorry. I thought you felt the same. I've been a total pillock; I got it wrong. And I promise; I'll never do it again. I promise, I won't touch you. Please, just let me drive you home. I won't say a word or make any kind of a move on you, I swear.'

I turned my head to look at him, with an icy steel gaze that he had never seen from me before. He looked perplexed and distraught, completely at a loss as to what just happened there. I spoke a little more sedately this time.

'Thanks for the offer, but I can't come with you. I'm going home on my own. Please don't follow me again.'

He was left standing there, totally bewildered.

As I walked off, I was so angry with myself. I was angry that I had allowed those feelings and emotions to be stirred up again. I had promised myself that I would bury them, for good, and no matter what happened, I wouldn't allow the past to dictate my present and future behaviour. But here I was—the first sign of male trouble, or rather the first sign of attention really, and I behave like some wild banshee. It begged the question whether I would ever trust any man, whether I would ever be able to allow any man to come near me, to touch me. Maybe there was some truth in what Mo said. Perhaps he was right, and I did have some feelings for him. He must have picked up on something. I liked being with him, I enjoyed his company, and we had a lot of fun together. But I had never indicated that I wanted anything more. It could never be anything other than platonic, because I could never bear the thought of being touched by any man ever again; even a man as lovely as Mo.

For the couple of weeks that followed, there was an awkward atmosphere between the two of us. We both felt uncomfortable about what had happened that evening. Thankfully, I had been distracted of late, as Henna had given birth to her baby, on the 28th of February, at five to midnight, just missing the dreaded leap year date: a gorgeous little boy, weighing in at only six pounds and three ounces, but perfectly formed all the same, who she named Kamran. We had been back and forth to Manchester to see the little man, and now he was already two weeks old. I loved being an aunty.

As we sat and waited for the verdict to be announced in one of the cases at the Crown Court, Mo finally broached the subject of the freezing cold mood that existed between the two of us. I had continued to ignore it, but he couldn't do it any longer. He wanted to clear the air; that much was obvious.

We found a quiet corner in the cafe, and went and sat with our coffees. Mo started by apologising again for trying to kiss me that evening.

'It's just that you properly freaked out at me that night. It was actually quite scary. I don't mean to pry but—'

'Then don't,' I darted in quickly before he could finish. I didn't want to go into it with him.

'Look, you don't need to explain yourself. That's not what I'm getting at. I just want to know if we can be friends again. Just friends, I won't expect anything more. I've really missed our banter these last couple of weeks, it's been so dull, us two not speaking properly. We usually have such a laugh; most of the day is a hoot when we are working together; so, how about it?'

I was messing around with the froth on my cappuccino as he spoke, and thought about it for a short while whilst I dragged the teaspoon back and forth. If I was truly honest, then I had to admit that I had missed it too. I had missed being with him, chatting about all the latest office and court gossip and goings on, mooting the finer points of the case, laughing and joking about our most recent mishaps. I had missed it all. I had missed him.

'Of course we can be friends,' I said, happy that we could go back to the way things were. Mo gave me an enormous smile, which told me everything about how he felt. I was just happy that things could get back to the way they had been.

Chapter 22: The final day

IT WAS 29ᵗʰ OF JUNE, and I couldn't believe it was here—my last day at the office. The final day was quite an emotional one for me. I had loved my time at Connors so much that I really, truly didn't want to leave. But I had always known it was temporary contract, and the lady who normally did the job was returning to her desk from her maternity leave, as had always been the understanding. There were no positions opening in the foreseeable future, but they said they would invite me to apply if anything came up. The disappointment remained nevertheless.

We all went for a drink after work, and Mo in particular made no bones about the fact that he was sad to see me go. After several lemonades and orange juices on my part, and several G&T's, beers, wines and vodkas consumed by most of the others, it was time to say my goodbyes to everyone. I was going to miss the place, and miss the people even more. They had all been so kind and welcoming, Rachel in particular, and of course Mo. I was never going to forget my time at Connors.

Mo offered to take me home, and we chatted on the way back to his car.

'What will you do now?' he asked, as he walked with his hands in his trouser pockets, whilst at the same time dragging his feet in the most laboured, drawn-out way imaginable. He was barely lifting his gaze off the pavement.

'I'm not really sure to be honest. I think I might register with an agency for some temp work, just admin stuff. Temping pays well for a start, and it's a good stopgap until I decide what I want to do with my life. I haven't really thought much beyond that at the moment.'

'You've done 'A' levels haven't you?' he asked.

'Yes.'

'What did you get if you don't mind me asking?'

'No, not at all, I got 3 A's,' I replied as we reached the car.

'Then, duh? Why didn't you go to university last year straight after sixth form?' Mo asked, with his palms out outstretched in amazement as to why in his opinion such a bright young lady like me hadn't done just that.

'It's complicated. I can't really tell you unless you have several hours to spare. Actually, make that a day or two!'

'Then maybe I will have to do just that. Let's not be strangers after you've gone. Let's keep in touch, and maybe meet up for a bite to eat sometime, just as friends that is.'

'I'd like that,' I replied, and I actually meant it. I had known Mo for almost six months now, and despite the one awkward incident, I now felt relaxed in his company.

He pulled up outside our house, which was miles away from his posh suburb on the other side of the city. I turned and looked at him with a tinge of regret as to what could have been if Zubair had not ruined my life.

'I'll be in touch. And thanks for everything,' I told him.

'No, thank you,' he said.

'What for?'

'For being a breath of fresh air Miss Selina Hussain. I'm going to miss you like crazy, but you know that, don't you? Don't you dare forget about me!'

'I won't,' I replied, and whereas I had once refused to get into his car, today I left it reluctantly.

Mo sat and wondered when he would see me again. The fact was that he would be seeing me much sooner than he could ever have imagined. However, nothing could ever have prepared him for the circumstances in which he would see me again.

Chapter 23: Dark Days Return

A WEEK AFTER LEAVING CONNORS, I started working at one of the branches of a local chain of high street insurance brokers on the other side of town. I was glad that the temping agency had managed to find me work so quickly. I had to take two buses to get there, but I didn't mind, as it was only temporary for three weeks. My job was simple, well in theory anyway, as I had to deal with pet insurance only. I didn't really know anything about pets, except for rabbits. I knew a bit about them. Henna and I had cried and begged for pets when we were younger. Adam was too young to join in, but I'm sure he would have, had he been able to talk. So my dad agreed to us having two rabbits in the back yard. We had gone with him to the pet shop and chosen two gorgeous, jet-black baby bunnies. They were Dutch lion-faced mini lops, and were completely adorable. My dad called them "Starsky and Hutch", after some cops in a television drama in the seventies that he used to watch. But that didn't matter as the rabbits themselves were beautiful. At first, they were fine. They used to cuddle up to each other, eat out of the same bowl, and play together for hours, binking around in the run. But then as they got older, they fought terribly. They had to be separated, and in reality, we weren't cut out for the amount of care and attention they required. And even though we loved them, we agreed to give them away to good homes where they would be looked after with the best care possible.

I wasn't sure how much my limited experience of pets would come in handy, but as it turned out, the work I had to do was all very straightforward. There was a list of questions I just rattled off, took the information down and clicked on the box to work out the quotation.

At the end of the first week, I arrived home to some bad news that I was completely unprepared for. My mum mentioned that Zubair was back from abroad, and she was going to visit him that evening. I went and sat down at the dining table, and my heart sank at the mere sound of his name. Just hearing the word "Zubair" made my head hurt. Whilst a few minutes ago I had been in reasonably good spirits, I now felt like the walls were closing in, and the room was dark and cold. She asked me if I wanted to come, but naturally I made up an excuse and got out of it. So far, I had evaded that man and was going to do everything possible to avoid seeing him again. I told her I was going to use the time to browse online and see if there were any good permanent jobs to be found.

A couple of hours later, I heard the front door shut as my mum arrived back from their house. As she walked in, she sounded all happy and excited. She called both me and Adam through to the living room.

'Look, Zubair *Bhai* brought some gifts for us all. How kind he is.' She handed Adam a pen displayed in a fancy box, with his name engraved on it, and showed us the red and green patterned silk scarf he had brought her. Then she pulled out of the bag what looked like a large and expensive perfume bottle. I didn't even touch it. I couldn't, and then she confirmed, as I had expected, that this was a gift for me. She told me it was an extremely expensive Arabian Oud perfume.

'Mum, I think this perfume isn't really right for someone my age. It's more of a mature fragrance. You have it.'

'Selina are you sure, you haven't even tried it. He bought it for you especially. That's what he said. Okay, if you are sure, but you have the scarf then.'

'No mum, I don't need that either. I've got plenty of scarves and perfumes, you keep them both. You never buy yourself anything, so it's only right that you should have them.'

'Well, if you insist.'

'I do. By the way mum, Uncle Sultan's son came and dropped the *mehndi* and wedding invitation cards for his daughter's wedding.'

Mum went and looked at the invites, which I had placed on the television stand. Obviously, she had already known the dates; the *mehndi* was this Friday evening, and the wedding on the Sunday. Asians always announced the dates verbally as soon as they were known, and then delivered the cards practically the day before. It was the Asian way of doing things. She commented on how pretty the cards were; the design of the bride in the *doli* was embossed onto the card, and the image of the palanquin sparkled with its glittery edges. 'They must have been printed in Pakistan', she declared. But she wasn't happy that the *mehndi* venue was quite far away.

'The *mehndi* hall is a bit of a distance, I've never actually been to this one before, although Mrs Begum says it is very nice and spacious, with a large stage. She thinks it used to be an old bingo hall that has been converted. I suppose all the ladies play bingo online now. Anyway, I don't know why they couldn't book anything nearer. But I think it is a joint *mehndi*, so maybe it is somewhere in the middle, because the boy is from Cleckheaton. Or is it Pontefract? I can't remember you know. So, what are you wearing to the henna night this Friday Selina? Adam has that lovely *sherwani* suit he has hardly worn; he can put that on. What about you?'

'I'm not going to go mum.' I said as I sat and flicked the television on.

'Not going to go? But why not? Everyone, and I mean everyone else is going to be there. You will enjoy it when you get there, all the music, and the dancing. Why don't you come? It will do you good, and you could do with a bit of a break. You know these *mehndis* are usually great fun, so colourful and lively. And I'm sure the food will be good too. Haji Sultan told me himself that they have booked Chilli Box as their caterers, for the *mehndi* and the wedding, and you know that right now they are the simply best around. Some of their dishes are just wonderful, especially their *reshmi* kebabs and their *ras malai.*'

'No, I really don't want to. I'm going to be so tired after a long week at work. I don't even get home until nearly seven, and that's when it starts. You and Adam go, honestly, I'll be fine at home.'

'Well, it's up to you darling. I'm not going to push you to go if you really don't want to. Oh, before I forget, Zubair was asking after you. And he said to make sure I tell you.'

I could feel my face becoming flushed, as there was an intense, protruding heat rising up my chest, all the way up my face and to the back of my head. I suddenly wanted to vomit.

'Tell me what mum?' I asked, trying to sound blasé, not moving my head, keeping my eyes fixed on the television.

'I told him you were on a temporary contract where you are now, and he said he knows that there is a really good admin job going at the University, and he can put in a good word which will mean the job is practically yours. But of course you do have to apply for it. He said he will drop the details off some time.'

'Please tell him there's no need. I'm happy temping at the moment.' My mind raced, trying to think of something good, something convincing to say, but this was all I had. I didn't know what else to say.

'*Beti*, temping is not really satisfactory. This is a permanent position, and I'm sure it would suit you. And the University is a good, respectable place to work. He says you could go and come back with him, in his car, which would be fantastic, so you wouldn't have to worry about catching the buses. And it is so kind of him to stick his neck out for you in this way. He didn't have to even mention it, but as usual, he is always trying to help this family in any way he can.'

I kept my eyes glued to the programme. There was a very glamorous looking chef, baking soft, light, fluffy croissants;

although she was so thin I don't believe she ever ate them herself. I was not really listening to what the cook was saying, but I could see they seemed like a lot of hard work.

'Well, if he calls, just take the stuff off him, please, and I will have a look at it when I get a chance,' I said, just to appease my mum so I would hear no more about it.

Chapter 25: Don't forget to lock the door

IT WAS FRIDAY EVENING, and sure enough, it was nearly seven o'clock when I walked through the door. I found that my mum was still at home, even though she should have left by now. She was in the living room, with her sewing machine out on the coffee table.

'What have you been sewing so late in the day mum?' I asked her as I walked into the living room briefly, before I went back out and dropped my bag in the hallway and hung up my coat. I looked at myself in the old mirror in the hallway. This mirror had seen better days. The frame was tatty round the edges now, and the surface was a little dull, with a few speckled grey spots here and there. It had hung here as long as I could remember, since the time I used to stretch myself tall to be able to see how my two plaits looked when I was ready for school in the morning. I never could see into it in the early years of primary school, so my dad used to lift me up, and I would hold my plaits in my hands right in front of me, and in particular, examine them to see that the pink ribbons were tied just right. I was very particular about those ribbons, and used to make my mum do them again and again until each bow was just as I had wanted it. Goodness, when I thought back, I had no idea how she had the patience! But when I gazed into this same old mirror today, I knew that phrase about the mirror not lying was sadly so true. I looked really tired; my eyes were dreary, and my skin was devoid of any kind of lustre. And inside I felt even worse. I was relieved not to be going to this *mehndi* function; I didn't think I would be able to keep my eyes open until the end, which was usually after midnight. Nor would I have been very good company.

I walked back into the living room. My mum was scouring the room. I knew she was looking for her handbag, which I picked up from the side of the sofa where she had been sewing.

'Your brother, he has ripped his *sherwani*. Can you believe it? I just noticed a little while ago when I got it out of the wardrobe. And you know the material is so stiff, I couldn't fix it by hand. Anyway, I've mended it now, and he's just getting changed.' As she finished speaking, Adam walked in looking very dapper in his traditional Asian attire.

'Whooo, don't you look handsome; not trying to impress anyone tonight are you? Not got a secret girlfriend we don't know about?' I teased him.

'Of course not; don't be stupid! I hate girls!' was his quite definite reply.

'Selina, don't be mean to him,' said my mum, feeling sorry for him, as she knew full well that Adam was so easy to wind up.

'The taxi's here mum. Come on, let's go,' he said, urging mum to make a move.

'Oh, okay, let's go, but Selina *beti* will you put the sewing machine and my sewing box away please? I haven't got time; we must leave now as we're already late. And don't forget to lock the door.'

'Yes, of course mum, I'll do it in a bit. You two get off and I will see you later.'

As they left for the front door, I went straight to the kitchen to put the kettle on. I looked in the fridge to see what there was to eat. There was some chicken *biryani* crammed into a plastic carton, and a bit of leftover pizza still in the cardboard box. After looking at them both for a few seconds, I decided that I wasn't really all that hungry yet, so I thought I would have a cup of tea instead. Perhaps it would perk me up a bit.

As I poured the water, I thought I heard a noise coming from the hallway, and went to have a look. Perhaps my coat had fallen off the hook. I walked to the hallway, but there didn't seem to be anything out of place. Remembering that I hadn't done it yet, I went over to go and lock the front door. It was when I was walking back to the kitchen that I heard his unmistakable voice.

'Hello Selina. Long time, no see.'

I looked into the living room and without even having moved a muscle I felt as though his voice catapulted me into an orbit of panic and suffocation. There he was, just standing there, larger than life, as if he owned the place.

'The front door wasn't locked. Honestly, Selina. You know you can't be too careful nowadays, can you?'

My eyes were fixed on him in panoramic terror, and my feet frozen to the ground where I stood in the doorway to the living room. I looked at him with utter incredulity. I didn't want to gawp at him, but I couldn't help it. My eyes wouldn't move. I was in a stupor of utter disbelief; he was there, right in front of me.

'Please leave,' I said in a pathetic, tiny voice. Imagine saying "please" to your rapist. But the fear was still there, an automatic, innate fear. I had never stopped feeling terrified of this man. My heart was beating faster than I had ever felt it, harder and harder, ramming against my chest. It was pounding like the echoing beat of loud, African drums. I was beginning to sweat with trepidation. The sweat turned my skin icy cold, and I was a shivering statue. I wanted him to go. I wished I had the strength to fling him out with my own bare hands. He had a menacing yet incredibly smug look on his face, and started coming toward me.

'Don't come any closer,' I said, my words barely managing to come out. And yet still, my legs were frozen to the spot. I couldn't move my legs. I was trying, but they wouldn't budge. What was wrong with me, aside from the fact that I was petrified of him? Why couldn't I move? I tried, but nothing. Why wasn't I able to run away, out of the house? Why wouldn't my legs work? Move, you stupid legs!

'Or what? What will you do?' he asked condescendingly. 'Anyway, I come in peace. Look, I've brought the details about that job. Your mother must have mentioned it to you. She was ever so grateful to me when I assured her I could get you the job.'

He tried to pass a brown envelope to me. I didn't move my hand to take it, so he placed it on the sofa next to where he was standing.

'Have you forgotten what I said to you? Let me remind you. You—are—mine. Do you understand? All of this drama you did, marrying that poor boy, what was his name? Ah, yes, Sohail. What was all that about? I knew it wouldn't come to anything. I told you that on your wedding day, didn't I? I said you would be back. And here you are! You cannot belong to anyone else, Selina. You will always and forever belong to me. You will do as I say, do you hear me!'

He grabbed my arm and started to pull me toward him. Yet again I felt like all the strength had vanished from inside my being. He dragged me into the living room. I tried to break free but his grip was too tight. Any fight I may have had inside me was gone. I was limp, and lifeless, all over again. He continued to drag me by the arm into the room, and soon, he had both my arms crossed tightly behind my back. He was bending over me and was trying desperately to kiss me. I struggled with whatever miniscule might I had, but I knew the inevitable. He had the same rage in his eyes as he'd had on that night. Those same putrid, demonic eyes were ablaze once again. Soon enough, he had me on the floor by the coffee table and was on top of me with full force. I cried, and tried to kick, and attempted a scream with as much energy as I could muster, but it was pitiful. My urge to scream the highest pitched scream ever just wouldn't materialise, as no sound would come out despite my efforts. My limbs were barely functioning.

'Please stop, please, please. I'm begging you, please!' I could speak, only just. It was more like a whisper. In any event, it made no difference.

Tick tock, tick tock, tick tock. I could hear it again. Banging in my head. It's all I could hear.

'No no no!' I said.

Tick tock, tick tock, tick tock. There was no clock in this room, yet it was gnawing at me, grinding me down.

Please God, no, I thought, I can't go through this again. I could smell his disgusting repulsive scent. Sweaty, woody, vile, like some filthy, revolting animal. No, he was worse than that. I couldn't even conjure up any words that could befit what I thought and felt about him. But I could think at least; my attempts to hit back, or yell, may have been feeble, but my thoughts hidden deep inside of me were running strong, free and wild.

Whilst he fiddled with his trousers, I managed to get one arm free. I reached out to grab the coffee table, and in the process my hand landed on my mum's scissors edging out of the sewing box. He suddenly brought his arm over my neck now, just under my chin, forcing my head rigidly into one place. Without thinking any further, I grabbed the scissors. With as much strength as I could galvanise, I somehow drew a colossal breath, deep down into my stomach, and as I breathed out, I plunged the scissors into the side of his neck as hard as I could; and as I did so I let out a huge, raucous scream. I heard the acrid tear of the skin as the sharp points of the scissors sliced open his neck. And then it stopped. It all ended. There was silence, and he was motionless as blood spurted out of his neck. His body was slumped on top of me; his head lay sideways next to mine. His wide-open eyeballs were next to my face. His eyes were fixed on me, protruding, silently trying to terrorise me still. I pulled myself away a little. His blood gushed out of his neck, cascading out as though it was water from a spring, and it was smothering him, me, the carpet. Blood on the carpet. Again. Stained. Yet again. But this stain was huge, and it continued to grow rapidly, in a pattern on the carpet all around his head. I will never be able to wash this much blood out of the carpet, I thought. Not this time. The crimson surge was spurting and pouring everywhere, but at least it did so quietly. All around me was silent. I could only hear my own breath, and could only feel my own heartbeat.

I wriggled out and away from him, stood up, and calmly looked down at his body. His eyes were still open, and his blood was still pouring out. And then it hit me. I was no longer crying, or shaking, and I was no longer fearful. I was no more frozen to the spot, as my legs had life in them again. So I walked over to the telephone, picked up the receiver and dialled 999.

'Emergency Services Operator, which service please?'

'The police please,' I said, noticing that my voice was now the epitome of perfect composure.

'Hello, Police. What is the problem?'

'My name is Selina Hussain. I live at 25 Hurst Street. I have just killed someone.'

'I'm sorry, can you repeat that?'

'My name is Selina Hussain. I live at 25 Hurst Street. I have just killed someone.'

'Are you at 25 Hurst Street now?'

'Yes.'

'And is the person you have killed, or think you have killed, there as well?'

'Yes.'

'Are you yourself hurt in any way?'

'No. I'm fine.'

'Please do not touch anything, stay where you are, the Police are on their way. What is the name of the person you think you have killed?'

'I don't *think* I have killed him; I *know* I have killed him. He is definitely dead. And his name is Zubair Qureshi.'

Chapter 26: A vision in white

I WENT AND UNLOCKED the front door in readiness for the arrival of the police, and then quietly came back and sat on the sofa, waiting patiently. I looked at his dead body and felt a monumental sense of relief. It was over. He couldn't hurt me again. I was free. I was finally free. This is what liberation felt like. Despite the bloody dead body that lay before me, I was at peace.

The police officers treated me pretty well considering I had just killed a man, and they quietly took me from the scene and marched me into the car. Mind you, it's not like I resisted them. Perhaps they were expecting someone a little hysterical, or weepy, or shaky, or emotional, or violent—or just anything; for I wasn't any of those things. I was calm and sedate, quiet and cooperative. The officers were visibly perplexed, and stared at me profusely.

I was at the police station within what seemed like minutes. And then the formalities commenced promptly. I was cautioned and read my rights. The Custody Sergeant was a burly fellow, with a thick moustache and a large, bald head. Did men keep moustaches, and indeed beards, to compensate? I wondered as I looked at him. The Custody Sergeant treated me respectfully, given the circumstances, and told me of my right to legal representation. I told him I didn't want to see the Duty Solicitor, but asked if he would contact Mo. He said he knew Mo very well; they all did at the station. He agreed to call Mo for me shortly, and he then told me about what was to happen next. So it followed—I had my personal items taken from me, I was fingerprinted and photographed, I had my clothing taken for forensics, and I was given a white suit to wear. I had my DNA samples taken, and was then asked to sign my charge sheet. The

Custody Sergeant did comment that I was the most forthcoming and helpful murder suspect he had ever dealt with, and I was the last sort of person he would expect to see in custody. I told him I didn't feel imprisoned, but rather, I felt like I had just been freed. His response was to scratch his bald head.

When he got the phone call, Mo moved faster than he had ever moved in his life. He was at the station in minutes, but as it turned out, he had to wait well over an hour before he could see me.

I was brought to the bare, colourless interview room, and we were left alone.

Mo looked at me with a decidedly blank expression on his face, as I walked in with my crisp, white onesie on; a vision in white. Well, perhaps not quite. My hair was dishevelled, and I still had bloodstains on my face and hands, but I didn't look as bad as he perhaps had thought I would. Maybe because I appeared calm, and didn't seem to be frightened, or sad, and wasn't tearful or nervous. He was more surprised by the fact that I displayed a gentle smile when I saw him. I think he was expecting me to start sobbing. I went and sat opposite him, and touched his arm gently. He sat there for a while, not saying anything, not knowing how to begin. I saved him the trouble.

'I'm really sorry to drag you out like this.'

He opened his mouth and closed it again.

'I didn't know who else to contact. Has anyone told my mum?'

'The police are still at your house, and they've filled her in on....on what's happened. It's a scene of crime, so the officers are still there taking fingerprints and photographs. Selina, what the bloody hell happened here? What in God's name have you done? Who was this man? And why have you killed him?'

He spoke with an air of astonishment, as he was clearly having trouble digesting it all. His green eyes looked at me disbelievingly, as if to say, "Did you really kill someone?"

'Mo, do you like me? As in, really like me, you know, care about me?'

'You know I do. I more than like you, and more than just care about you. I think that much is obvious, isn't it?'

'Then are you sure you want to hear this? I won't mind if you don't want to, and I won't blame you. I can always ask for the Duty Solicitor if you're uncomfortable with it. I don't want to put you through this unless you're absolutely sure you can hack it.'

Mo took a deep breath before he replied. 'Whatever it is, I can take it, and yes I do. I do want to hear what you've got to say. And I want to help you.'

'That man that I killed today, his name is Zubair Qureshi. He is a good friend of the family. He's a real pillar of the community; highly educated, well liked, respected, an honourable man,' I said, with a caustic tone in my voice which he couldn't help but notice. He raised his eyebrows.

'According to everyone I know, that is. He is, was, a fatherly sort of figure, very kind, religious, a friend to all, so helpful and charitable. He can't, I mean, he couldn't, put a foot wrong, ever. Almost a saint wouldn't you say?' Mo sat with his arms crossed as I spoke, listening quietly, his worried gaze fixed on me all the while.

'Not true,' I continued. 'That thing that I killed today was not a man; he wasn't even worthy of being called a human being. He was an evil sexual predator. He was trusted completely, wholeheartedly, by my mum, and by everyone who knew him, the whole stupid community. But I knew what he was really like.'

'Go on,' he urged me, nervously rubbing the back of his neck, fearful of what was coming next.

'Last summer, I was struggling with my Economics, and as he had done a degree in the subject and taught some aspects of it at University, he offered to give me some lessons, in readiness for my 'A' level exams. My mum was so grateful to him, as ever. He had been a true tower of strength the year before when my dad had died, seeing to everything at the mosque and so on. And here he was, helping our family, yet again, out of the kindness of his heart. So anyway, the one evening, his wife wasn't in. And so he....'

I paused for what seemed like an eternity, but must have only been a minute.

'He? He what, Selina?'

It was still so damned difficult to talk about.

'He, he.....he raped me. But I never told anyone about it.'

Mo looked at me with utter horror and disbelief slapped right across his face. He then turned his head away for a few moments.

'Why didn't you go to the police?' he said, turning to look back at me.

An obvious question, an obvious step, I thought; obvious to someone like Mo. But, as I explained to him, it was not so obvious to a young, vulnerable eighteen- year old woman who still very much felt like a girl, or at least she had done up until this point. A girl with a widowed mother, who along with everyone else, thought the sun shone from this man's backside and probably every other orifice. Not so obvious to a girl who people already thought was a bit of a lush, hanging out with boys instead of going to school, and who was confused as to whether she might be in some way to blame, and thought people would assume she was to blame. Not that obvious to a girl who had been threatened by this man, a man she was petrified of, a man that she feared would make *her* look like the perpetrator and bring shame to her mother's door and to her father's honourable memory if she breathed a word.

'Going to the police and standing up in court to testify would have had exactly the same effect; I would have to be cross examined and have to publicly relive the whole wretched shameful ordeal in front of strangers. That would be just as much *besti*. More than me or my mum could bear,' I told him. 'Not such an obvious step for a young girl like me who was scared and felt alone, with no one she could turn to.'

Mo thought about what I said for a little while. He knew enough about the community I lived in to understand my apprehension in taking that huge, bold step, and deep down, he did kind of get it. In hindsight, it may have been the right thing to do at the time, but it never felt like it was a decision that that I was strong enough to take *at that time.*

I then told him about the baby, and Sohail, and the miscarriage, and how we were now separated. And I went through what happened tonight; as plainly and as simply as I could.

'Sure enough, I was shocked to see him at my house, as he had crept in uninvited and had taken me by surprise. But I had no intention of killing him when I first saw him this evening. Nor did I ever think of anything like that at any time in the past. But equally, or perhaps more so, I also had no intention of being raped again. And if the sharp scissors had not been there, then that is exactly what would have happened to me today. He would have raped me. Again. I am absolutely sure of that.'

Mo could barely listen, and he held his head in his hands through much of it. He was staggered that I had hidden so much pain and heartache from him, from everyone. 'I've known you for six months. It hurts to learn that I never really knew you at all,' he said, in a hushed tone.

Despite this, he was adamant that he would do whatever it took to help me. His eyes belied his outward professionalism. His beautiful, mellow, green eyes gave it away. That he cared deeply for me. I feared that perhaps he even loved me.

Chapter 27: Tears on my pillow

THE POLICE INTERVIEW that followed my meeting with Mo was awash with questions for which I didn't have any logical answers as far as the officers were concerned. Mo had told me I could remain silent, but I no longer had anything to hide or fear. Zubair was dead. I could tell the truth as boldly as I wished, for he couldn't frighten me anymore. But my truth just didn't sound so good out aloud, especially to two, hardened cops whose sole aim was to trip me up, and then some. The lady officer was looking at me, nose perched high in the air, with an air of indignation that made me feel uneasy. It didn't help that she had the biggest, most bulging eyes I had ever seen. And they were a piercing, an icy blue that went straight through me. She had a cold, drawn-out voice to match her cold persona. Every sentence she spoke seemed to drag on and on. Her sidekick was a man a few years younger than her, with an odd, almost blank expression on his square-shaped, spotty face that I could not fathom. His countenance gave nothing away, good or bad.

I went round and round in circles about the rape, and the reasons why I hadn't reported it. They dismissed my honour and *besti* tribulations, and the fact that I was petrified of him. I dug myself deeper and deeper, trying to convince them that I was certain that he was going to rape me once more and that was why I killed him. I killed him to defend myself from the inevitable attack. At the end of it all, I was exhausted. I think perhaps they decided to end the interview more because they were also tired themselves, rather than the fact that they felt sorry for me. So they decided to call it a day.

A not-so-kind police officer led me down the bare, imageless corridors to my cell and shoved me into it very ungraciously. He slammed the door shut. I stood still where my feet had landed after I was pushed in. I looked around in what must have been a box no bigger than the stationary cupboard at Connors. The room was tiled from top to bottom. The colour of the cell consisted of varying shades of grey, with an air of foreboding that filtered right through and into my head as if to remind me of where I actually was, in case I thought I was dreaming. There was a bench opposite me against the wall, topped with what I guessed was a blue mattress, but it actually looked like a gym mat. It had been ripped here and there, and there were bits of the foam poking out. I trundled over and sat down. The room smelled. The stationary cupboard at Connors smelt nice; of brand new envelopes and starchy, white paper. This smelled rank. It smelled of other people; of their pee and sweat and tears. I was sure many tears had been shed on this blue gym mat. I slowly lay on my side and pulled my knees to my chest, my body now beginning to feel cold with the realisation of where I was; all alone in a tiny, foul-smelling room with no windows, in which I felt I couldn't breathe. My mum always smelled nice. That's one thing all us kids used to agree on. We used to tell our dad that he never smelled as good as her. She had the "mum" smell—warm, cosy, comforting. Mum! I want my mum, I said to myself, as my tears rolled off my cheeks and fell on to the blue gym mat.

Chapter 28: My new abode

DESPITE THE BEST EFFORTS of my defence team, I was remanded in custody. The Crown Prosecution Service managed to convince the Judge that bearing in mind the violent nature of the killing, and the fact that the murder happened at the Defendant's own home, which was in close proximity to the victim's house in a community where feelings were running high, the most preferred and safest option, particularly having regard to the deceased's widow and his sons who lived in the neighbourhood, would be to deny bail to Selina Hussain.

I couldn't bear to look at the Judge as he gave his severe, cold decision, in his deep, highly polished voice, to incarcerate me until the trial. Did he have a heart? Did he have any kids? Any daughters? How easily he said those words. How easily he sent me away. I couldn't look at my mum as she sat in the public gallery. I knew for a fact that she was crying; I caught a glimpse from the corner of my eye, even though I tried my damndest to avoid seeing her. I glanced at Mo as I was being led down. His face was the depiction of an image of gloom that I had never seen in him before, and when it boiled down to it, my mother's anguish, and Mo's pain, all of it, was because of me.

I was remanded to Ridings Hall Prison, a closed women's prison in North Yorkshire, about thirty or forty miles north of Leeds. The journey to the prison seemed to be long and laborious; mainly as I could not think of one positive thing the whole time that I sat in the van. I sat with my eyes closed for most of the journey, wondering when the vehicle would finally stop, and put me out of my misery as I thought about the prison I was being taken to. I had been there once before, but when I had worked at Connors, sitting on the other side. I had never actually seen the cells, just an interview room. I felt the dread physically regurgitating in the pit of my stomach, churning away. In reality, the ride there didn't take all that long; it was only just under an hour before I arrived. I was fortunate enough to be led to a cell, which I discovered I was to have all to myself, at least for now. I had not been looking forward to the prospect of having to share, of having to explain why I was there and what I had done. I would have to do that enough at the trial.

My cell was small and blank—I had never seen a room so depressingly, hideously ugly in all my life. It consisted of plain, grubby walls, a plain, hard floor, metal bunk beds, a desk and a chair. It was so tired looking, much like me at the moment. I lay on the bottom bunk and closed my eyes, knowing I had to come to terms with the fact that this was my new home for the foreseeable. I could hear noises coming from the other cells, and shouting from a distance. It seemed, from what I could make out of the shouts and screams, like there was some trouble with a prisoner, and the guard was dealing with it very loudly. I was told that I wouldn't get any trouble from other inmates because murdering a rapist earned you great admiration, and although that was some consolation, it couldn't detract from the fact was that I was locked up and had no idea if and when I would be freed. Although I knew how I had got here, because of that fiend, I gave myself a migraine wondering how I was going to get out. Suddenly, I missed my home and my family, and apart from the sense of loss I had felt when my dad had died, I missed it more than I had ever missed anything in my whole life.

The matter was transferred to the Crown Court and the team at Connors began in earnest to try and build up the case for my defence. But they came across stumbling blocks again and again, as Mo, acting as my solicitor, and my barrister,

David Evans, who I had met that very first time that I had gone to court with Mo, explained to me on a prison visit. As we sat in our allotted legal representatives' room going over everything, David played devil's advocate. There were so many holes in my case.

'So, Selina. You were attacked by Mr Qureshi on the 14th of June last year, is that correct?'

'Yes, I've been through all this.' I sounded obnoxious, but that wasn't my intention. I was just so tired. I couldn't sleep in that excuse of a bed, which felt like lying on a sack of stones. I wanted my own soft, comfy bed, with my beautiful scatter cushions and cuddly teddies.

'Yes, I know, but we are going to do it all over again. And again, and again. So, you were raped, and yet you managed to go home, you went upstairs to your room and didn't tell a soul. You didn't tell your family, not even your mother, nor did you mention it to any of your friends, no one at all. Why didn't you phone the police?'

'I've already said, I was scared. He threatened me. He said he would humiliate me and my family. Everyone adored him. They still do. I'm sure when they find out what I am accusing him of, pretty much all the people who knew him will think I'm making it up. They think he's like Mr Perfect or something.'

'Okay, so you couldn't tell the police, or your mum because of these honour issues; but what about a friend? Or a teacher? Or anyone. Didn't you have any friends?' David asked firmly.

'Of course I had friends, and one really close friend, Abigail. But I was having exams at the time, and she went abroad. And then, I went along with the marriage to Sohail and moved to Birmingham. After I lost the baby and came back to my mum's house, she was off at university, and I didn't see any point in bothering her or anyone else about it. More to the point I just didn't want to talk about it to anyone. I wanted to forget about it, just put it out of my head. Can't you see that? I mean, why on earth would I want to chat about something like that to anyone? And what would it have achieved? It's not something you can just blurt out, oh hey, by the way, I forgot to say, I was raped!'

David stood with one arm across his body, his chin resting on the hand of his other arm, and thought for a minute or so. He then leaned over the table.

'You see, the trouble is that normally, with an allegation of rape, it would be your word against his. But the problem we have here is that he is dead. We have absolutely no independent evidence, no witnesses, no forensics that would prove that he raped you. By your own admission, you lied to Sohail by not telling him that you were pregnant when you married him, and then you were going to pretend it was his baby. So you are admitting that about yourself, acknowledging that you are very well capable of deceit. That's something the Prosecution will have a field day with, as you will be doing their work for them. And what's more you have absolutely no proof that he was the father of the baby. We can't even prove that sex took place, never mind that he raped you and you fell pregnant. Even if we could prove the paternity, which we can't, but even if we could, there is still no evidence that he raped you. You were not under age at the time, and there is nothing to disprove that you consented to having sex with him.'

'How many times do I have to say this. I didn't consent to sex with him; he raped me!' I shouted with my hands in the air, an act of blatant exasperation.

'Selina, please don't get all irate and upset, we are trying to help you. You have got to get your head around what you're up against, what we're all up against,' said Mo, trying desperately to calm me down. 'We've been doing our research and asking around, and no one in that neighbourhood has a bad word to say about him, nor does anyone at his place of work. And as far as I'm aware, his laptop, mobile phone, computers at home and work, they've all been checked by the police, and there is nothing incriminating on them.'

'And the CPS statements don't help your case at all,' added David quickly, as if he was keen not to lose the momentum whilst they had my attention. 'His wife seems to be suggesting that you in fact had a bit of a thing about him, and *he* cancelled the rest of your lessons because you made a play for him and he knocked you back. She says that when she got back home that night, he told her he wasn't going to teach you anymore, and the reason was a bit embarrassing because you made it obvious you had a crush on him. Apparently, according to her, you wouldn't leave him alone *even on your own wedding day.* You called him up to your bedroom. So, in a nutshell, she is saying you tried it on with him and he declined your advances.'

I rolled my eyes upon hearing this, and then dropped my head in my hands in disbelief. After a few moments I looked up and was ready to charge.

'That's nonsense. I cancelled the rest of the revision sessions because of his attack on me. And he just came up to my bedroom on my wedding day, I didn't invite him up, I didn't want to see him ever again. That's the reason why I wanted to marry and move away, to get away from him. And if he was trying to keep away then why did he come round that night, the night I killed him. His excuse was about some job for me, but really he just wanted to have his wicked way with me again. Don't you see, he got off on it, living dangerously like that, so close to a knife edge; everyone thinking he was some pious angelic person while all the time he was a deranged, demonic devil. It gave him power, power over me. He was mental, bloody deranged he was, why doesn't anyone believe me?'

'It only matters that the jury believe you,' said David. 'His wife says that your mum had told him how you were working at some insurance firm miles away, and *she* had asked *him* if he knew of any jobs going. Note that it wasn't the other way around. So he told her about the job at the university. We've checked that out, there was a job going and the details were indeed in the envelope, which the police recovered from the scene. He told his wife that he was going to drop the envelope off at your house on his way back from work. His wife recalls that he said he would go to your house on that particular evening and just push it through the letterbox because he knew you would be out with your family at the function that they were indeed at, only of course you didn't go. We can't find any disparity in any of that so far. So we now have to convince the jury that when he came in he tried to attack you, and that you acted in self-defence, to stop him from raping you.'

'Well, why else would I kill him, I mean, think about it, I have no reason to want him dead other than what I have told you.'

'The Prosecution can present any scenario they want,' said Mo.

'That's right,' added David, 'the most obvious one being that you were in a jealous rage at the time, because you wanted him, and he didn't want you, so you killed him. His wife is quite adamant that you were smitten with him. They could argue that after your marriage broke up and you came back, you wanted to have some sort of relationship with him, but he refused. They could say that was the reason why he ended up dead. So far, this guy has come up more squeaky-clean than the Pope, so unless we can get something on him quickly, we are going to have an almighty uphill struggle. On the night of his death, your clothes weren't ripped, your hair hadn't been pulled, and you didn't have any cuts or bruises. There is no tangible evidence of a struggle, and certainly no evidence of anything of a sexual nature having gone on in there. The only blood that was shed was his. And the only evidence that exists is a pair of scissors in his neck, which you have admitted that you put there. You can see where I am going with this, can't you?'

I slumped back in my chair, teary-eyed and exhausted. It seemed as though a whirlpool of angst and negativity had taken root in my head, swirling around. My mind and body both ached. I was beyond tired.

'I'm really shattered; I can't do this anymore. Please, no more today. I want to go now.'

Chapter 29: Where am I?

WHERE AM I? I ask myself the same question again. I am wearing a pure, white, floor-length dress, made of beautiful, soft silk, with thin, white chiffon sleeves that are fluttering in the slight breeze. There is a hint of a shimmer to it, which catches the eye as the moon shines down from the blanket of midnight blue sky that is dotted with an abundance of twinkling stars. It's quite dark, and I am standing all alone; but where, I ask myself as I turn my attention away from the moonlit sky and survey what is around me..... I'm in the park. Ah, yes; the park. I smile and start to reminisce. This is the beautiful park that I practically lived in during my childhood. Climbing, or trying to climb, the trees. Well, the smaller ones anyway. I see myself feeding the ducks in the lake. Having competitions on the swings to see who could go the highest. I think about my time here with my sister, and all our friends, from around the age of five right up to our early teens, when we used to ride our bikes and scooters and play rounders. And we loved a game of cricket. Cricket wasn't just for boys, my dad would tell me. Yes, I can see and hear it all. I used to love the 'crack', that unmistakable sound of the ball hitting the bat. My dad was great at cricket, especially spin bowling. He knew his googlies from his *doosras*. And he even knew all about the *theesra*. He said forget all the others. Pakistan's Abdul Qadir was the best spin bowler the world had ever seen, and ever will see: the Wizard. That's what they called him. I remembered seeing some of his amazing bowling on You Tube with my dad, watching his curly locks flow back and forth as he bowled such twisters that even the world's best batsmen used to get themselves in a pickle. We would both of us sit on the sofa munching on freshly-roasted monkey nuts, which had been sent over from Pakistan, straight from the family fields in the village. It was the closest you could get to the soil of that land, without actually eating it, is what my mum used to say.

But wait, where am I now? I'm not with my mum and dad. Oh yes, in the park. I'm back in the park. But why am I in the park? Why am I not at home? I should go home, it's very late. I'm not allowed to be in the park so late. I turn around and look at the lake, which is down the slight hill, and then I look further into the distance, and I can still just about make out the woods. But I hear something. What's that noise? It's coming from behind me. I slowly turn around. I don't believe it! It's Zubair! Only it's not. It's Zubair's *head*! It is just his head. Where has his body gone? His neck is still there. Oh his neck, his neck, the scissors are stuck in his neck! It is dripping with blood; it just keeps pouring right down onto the ground. The green grass is stained. Stained! The patch of red on the grass is growing. His eyes are big and open wide, and piercingly positioned on me. They keep staring, and staring. He opens his mouth to speak, but only blood gushes out. My heart is thumping, and my head is pounding. He is going to get that blood on my dress! My pure, white, untouched dress will be ruined! Run Selina, run! I tell myself again—run! Run for your life! I can't! 'Tick tock, tick tock, tock,' he says as the head continues to focus on me, the blood still dribbling down. I can't move, my feet won't move! I yell at myself. The head starts floating along in the air toward me. I am now grabbing my legs with both my hands, yanking them ferociously. I keep pulling at my legs, and finally, finally, I am running. Go Selina, fly like a kite; fly away! The head picks up speed, gliding through the air after me like some supersonic jet, still dripping with blood, and still repeating 'tick tock, tick tock, tick tock.' I run faster, I'm tearing away now, faster than ever, as this is a race I *have to* win. Oh no! No! I didn't see it. I've run straight into it, and fallen in. Fallen in the lake. I look up, and the head is above me. I can't breathe. I'm going down, slowly, slowly, down I go. The kite is sinking. I close my eyes, and I can't hear or see anything. Finally, it is darkness. Blackness. Silence. There is nothing to see, and nothing to hear. I am sinking, deeper, deeper....

I awake with both my hands wrapped around my neck. I am covered in sweat, and I really can't breathe! I gasp for air, and then turn over, almost choking, and for a few seconds more, I feel as though I am still drowning.

It was a bad dream, I tell myself. Wake up Selina! It was just a nightmare. Slowly my breath starts to come a little more evenly. Slowly I sit up straighter and look around me. I am in my prison cell. I am alive. I can still see. And I can still hear. So I am still drowning.

Chapter 30: Home truths

THE DAYS AND WEEKS passed with a painstaking slowness that I couldn't get my head around. I would lie on the bed, or sit on the chair, with my eyes fixed on one scabby piece of wall, for what seemed like ages, only to realise that just ten minutes had passed. Time took on a new meaning. Where before there had never been enough time for anything, now I had an abundance of it that made me sick to my stomach. The day slowly chased away the night, and the night equally slowly chased away the day. I existed in a repetitive trance. Each day melted into the next without any meaning or purpose.

It was almost six weeks before I was mentally in a position to agree to see my mum. Contrary to the three one-hour visits a week that I was allowed the privilege of as a prisoner on remand, I told my mum that I only wanted to see her once, and once only, and under no circumstances was she to bring Adam, or Henna. I figured I at least owed her that, but I couldn't bear the thought of her seeing me like this week in week out.

I lay on my lumpy bed on the bottom bunk that morning, in anticipation of my mother's impending visit, gazing at my usual scabby piece of wall; dirty, shady grey, with sporadic specks of black. Not at all pleasing to look at, but my eyes always fell on it anyway.

I had absolutely no clue as to how this was going to go. Would she be angry? She would probably be angry alright. Would she be sad? Would she care about me, or care more about the scandal? I thought back to all the times when I had the opportunity to tell her what Zubair had done, and chose not to. I was now paying for that indecision.

As I walked into the visiting room, she was sitting there, appearing fragile and distinctly out of place. She really looked like she was finding just the act of sitting in this room excruciating. But thankfully she was alone, just as I had asked. She had one of her pretty *salwar kameez* suits on. This one had always been one of my favourites; a soothing dusky pink in colour, with tiny lavender blue flowers dotted along the neckline and hemline. She had the pink georgette scarf wrapped around her head loosely, as she always did when she was out of the house. She looked up at me as I approached her and she couldn't disguise the shock in her face. Perhaps it was the way I looked, or maybe just the fact that I was locked up, and for the first time in the family's history she was visiting someone in prison. Only, it was not just any old person; it was her own daughter.

'How are you mum?' I asked slowly, as I took a seat opposite her. It was evident how she was from the red, puffy eyes encased with dark circles around them.

'How do you think I am? Anyway, look at you Selina. You have lost so much weight. You are a shadow of yourself.' My mum spoke with a shiver in her voice, trying to suppress the tears that were all so ready to come out without much invitation.

'Well, the food's not as good as yours for a start. It's not too bad actually, all things considered.'

'What about the other prisoners, they don't give you any trouble do they? You hear about it on the news, how prisoners get bullied and attacked all the time.'

'No mum, it's just the opposite. It's kind of strange and a bit unbelievable, but as far as they're concerned, I killed a rapist, so in other words I eliminated a piece of scum from the planet, and I get top respect.'

'Respect? Respect? Do you call this respect?' my mum asked, wagging a finger as she did so, just like she used to when we were kids and we had done something naughty.

'Mum, I did what I had to do because I had no choice.'

'You killed a man, Selina! You killed Zubair *bhai*!' She was now beginning to become angry as she spoke.

'He was no brother to you. Your brother would not have raped me, would he?'

'Stop!' My mum said, putting her hands to her ears. 'I can't listen to this!'

'Well you are going to have to. It is time to stop burying you head in the sand. I tried that, and believe me, it doesn't work. You're going to have to endure this and hear what I have to say. On the evening of the last lesson I had, your precious Zubair attacked me. I got pregnant, and that is why I went through with the wedding to Sohail. I did it to keep the family's *izzat* and to make you happy. I'm sorry mum, maybe I should have told you at the time, but honestly, what would you have done?'

My mum was now sobbing quietly, finding this whole conversation every bit as difficult as I had anticipated. Perhaps even more so.

'Still, you should have come to me,' she said, pulling an old, green-coloured, paper napkin out of her jacket pocket and wiping her tears. It was probably one she had picked up at a wedding or some other gathering. 'You should have told me. Why did you assume that I wouldn't have believed you? I am well aware of what men can be like you know.'

She looked away as she spoke those last few words, deliberately avoiding eye contact with me.

'What do you mean by that mum?'

'Nothing, it doesn't matter.'

'Of course it matters, mum, tell me, what are you talking about?'

Still, she gave no details, and tried to brush it off as just something you say, that she didn't mean anything by it. But I knew there was more to it than that.

'Mum. Please.' I implored her again, trying not to raise my voice.

She gave a little sigh, and took a few deep breaths.

'I was not even seventeen when I married your father. He was twenty-two years of age. As you know, I lived in Pakistan. He had been raised here, but it was always his father's wish that he should marry me, as I was the only daughter of his only brother. In those days, this was seen as an ideal match, cousins getting married, and it is still seen like that by a lot of people even now, but less so I guess. I was well educated for my age, was considered a bright and conscientious student, and spoke good English. Your grandfather said I was very pretty, very domesticated and well raised, so he and your grandmother were very pleased to make the *rishta*. When your father came over to Pakistan, I assumed he was happy, too. He never said anything different to me or anyone else. But he only came over literally for the wedding, staying just a couple of days, and said he had to rush back for his work. He worked in a bakery at that time, and he said it was a busy time of the year, and he would lose his job if he didn't get back quickly. Anyway, when I came over, I soon realised that your father was not happy with our union. I was his wife, but he barely spoke to me. He was hardly ever at home. He didn't even touch me. We had no husband-wife relationship at all.'

My mum twisted the green napkin around in her hands whilst she spoke, looking down as she did so. I listened quietly, and watched the sorrow gather in my mum's face. She went on.

'Well, how do you think I felt? I may have lived in a village in Pakistan, and we may not have been rich, but we weren't poor either, and above all I was happy, so happy over there. My dad worked hard, as did my brothers, and with their help, and with the assistance of your granddad from England in meeting some of the expenses, my dad allowed me to go to a prestigious school in Rawalpindi. It was an hour's drive each way, and my mum worried terribly because there were always such awful accidents on the GT Road almost every day. But as far as I was concerned, I was living the dream. I loved it. I went to a fantastic school and had a happy life. I still remember the smells and sounds of my journey as though it were yesterday. I spent my days at school actually enjoying and appreciating my lessons, and having such a wonderful time with my class fellows, girls who I had genuine, affectionate friendships with. And the rest of my time, after I had done my homework, I spent chasing chickens, collecting the eggs, picking peanuts from the fields, shopping for bangles and the latest *salwar* suits, and making the *rotis*. But I was blissfully content with my life over there. I got the top grades in my class three years in a row before I came here, and was told by the Principal that I had the potential to go to University and do medicine if I continued with my studies. And I was part of a loving family, parents who doted on me as their only daughter and brothers who spoilt me. So it was a complete shock for me to come here and feel so lonely. I had no one. Don't get me wrong, your grandparents were not bad to me, they were good in their own way, but they couldn't take the place of a husband. They felt bad, but they couldn't change anything. I found out in the fullness of time that actually your father was in love with, and in a relationship with an English lady, called Jennifer. They had met at work, and he had been seeing her for a few years. He never wanted to marry me in the first place, but he didn't have the guts to stick up to his dad. So he went through with the wedding just to make his parents happy, but he carried on with Jennifer right where he had left off as soon as he got back to England. The only one who really lost out was me. His parents had a daughter-in-law to run around after them, cooking three meals a day and cleaning the house top to bottom, and he had his mistress to comfort him. I would cry myself to sleep at night, all alone in my bed, whilst he was over at Jennifer's, leading a double life. Well, you can imagine it for yourself. Anyway, after a good few years of not having a grandchild, your grandfather started putting pressure on your father, and he made it clear that he expected a grandchild, and more specifically a grandson, in his lifetime, or else his line would end, and he was not having that. So, in the end, your father relented once again to appease his dad. And so your father, well, he....you know. How do you imagine I felt? That this man, who I had married with a clean heart to start a new life as his companion, who I had given up a bright future in Pakistan for, only deigned to sleep with me because his dad had ordered him to. I felt used, unappreciated, dirty even, like I was just some means to an end. So, the babies came, and finally everybody got their boy when Adam was born.'

'But mum, you and dad never seemed that unhappy. I don't remember it anyway,' I said to her, unsure as to why I felt the need to make this statement. I guess I just didn't want to believe this about my dad, who I thought had been so perfect, a great human being. I didn't recognise this version of my father at all.

'Well, there was a peculiar twist in the fate of this story. When Adam was just a baby, and you girls were both quite young as well, Jennifer died unexpectedly, in a car crash. How ironic, don't you think? That he should go in the same way. Like true love, wouldn't you say? I don't need to say how upset your father was at the news of her sudden death. It took him a few years before he even began to try to get over it. He never really did, you know, but I think the absence of Jennifer made him look inwards toward his own family. At first, I think he just clung on to you three, but as time went by, he grew a little affectionate toward me also, and began to appreciate everything that I had done; for all of you children, for both his parents, and for him. He finally seemed to acknowledge the fact that I had devoted all my life to the home and family. But do you know what the worst thing was? No matter what he did, it was too late. However beautiful the gifts or words, it didn't matter anymore. Sure, I smiled through it all, put up a front, and never reproached him, never fought over it, but there was a big silent hole in my heart that just wouldn't mend. Whereas once upon a time, I would have been the happiest woman in the world had I received such affection from him, by the time it came, after so many years, it had no effect, and I couldn't love him. I respected him, was kind to him, but I couldn't love him.'

I was dumbstruck. I had no inkling about this history concerning my parents. I looked at my mother pensively, and thought what a brave soul she was. And what a selfless human being she was. She never, not even once, let on about how badly she had been done by. How hard it must have been for her. I had always thought my dad was perfect, almost to the exclusion of my mum. I had been so unfair to her. I felt a surge of regret wash through me. I wish I had known.

My mum's gaze softened, as she gently took my hands in hers.

'I believe you Selina. I believe you. I wish you had felt able to come to me. And I am so, so sorry that I put you in that position for this to happen to you. I didn't know what he was like,' she said, the tears gathering in her eyes again.

'Mum, it's not your fault. How could you have known? None of us did. Everyone still thinks he was some kind of a saint. Please don't blame yourself; the only one to blame is him.'

'Selina, please let me come and see you again. And Adam is missing you terribly. He's so confused.'

'Mum, I am sorry, but I can't let you come to this place again and again to see me like this. And bringing Adam here is not even an option. Please mum, you have to see it from my point of view. It's not only to protect you, but me too; every time I see you, saying goodbye will become harder and harder.

It will be like torture. Whatever will be, will be; I'm putting everything in Allah's hands now. This thing is beyond my comprehension. I need a miracle to save me now.'

Chapter 31: A companion

IT WAS LATE MORNING, and I was lying in my bed and for a change staring at the photo of my family on the wall instead of the grubby grey patch. The image was from happier times, all five of us on Blackpool Beach on a warm summer's day, Blackpool Tower visible in the background. I must have been about thirteen years old. I looked blissfully happy as I stood there, feet submerged in the sandy water, with my two, long plaits dangling down, and my round, rosy cheeks shining. I was just coming out of my slightly chubby phase. By the following year, I had shed all my puppy fat.

I heard the door to my cell fling open, startling me enough to make me turn and sit up.

'Morning Selina,' said the Prison Guard Angie, as she walked in behind another woman who was dragging her feet as she entered the cell. 'This is your new roommate. Selina meet Dorothy. Dorothy, meet Selina. Right, I shall leave you to it. Play nicely girls.'

The door clanged shut, and for a few seconds, we just looked at each other. She must have been in her late fifties, I thought, maybe even early sixties. She was quite short, and on the fat side. She had a pale complexion, and had an equally pale blonde, slightly unruly, shoulder-length mop of hair.

'Call me Dotty,' she said as she walked over and sat on the chair next to the bunk. 'You got a nickname?'

'No. I'm just Selina. Pleased to meet you—.' I stuck out my hand, but I don't think she even noticed it, as she looked around the cell with a fine squint at every little detail, not that there was much to look at.

'Likewise,' she replied, her eyes still perusing the cell around her, and there was another small silence. 'You got the bottom bunk I see.'

I looked at her large frame, and didn't hesitate. 'You can have the bottom one. I fancied a change anyway.'

I had never shared a room with a stranger before. I was secretly dreading it, but I needn't have worried, for we became friends quite quickly.

Dotty was full of admiration when I told her my story.

'Well, you're a brave lass, I'll give you that. You'd never believe it to look at you. You're such a tiny, skinny, delicate looking thing. You look like you'd fall over if I blew on you.'

I gave out a small, schoolgirl-like giggle, and that was something I hadn't done in a while.

'So why are you here?' I asked.

'Well, I've been an idiot, I have, pure and simple. If only I could turn back the clock and not make the dumb decision that I did.'

'What did you do?' I was intrigued as to why someone who looked like a granny was in a prison like this.

'I'm a cleaner you see, clean all these posh houses, mainly in Ilkley and places like that, you know, where all the rich folk live. Not like me. I live in one of the not-so-posh parts of Leeds. Same for my daughter and her kids; they live about ten minutes from me. Anyway, my granddaughter, Jess, brought home a letter from school for a trip to Spain. My daughter can't afford to send her on trips like that; I mean, she has two younger boys, so money is always tight. Her husband buggered off with another woman when the little one was only one. So I said I'd try to help. But I don't have two pennies to rub together myself. There's this one old lady I clean for, she has a massive house. She's absolutely loaded, she is, and so miserly with it. I really felt bad for Jess, she wanted to go so much, and she and her brothers miss out on a lot in life, on account of my daughter having to live off the pittance she gets paid for her part-time job and a few scrappy pieces of benefits payments. Anyway, this old lady was out the one day, or at least I thought she was out, so I figured why not take some money from her stash upstairs, she'd probably never even notice. She keeps cash hidden away in this drawer in a dresser in one of the bedrooms, but she never uses it. I know because it's always there, every week. Maybe it was her emergency money or something. And I wasn't stealing it really, I was borrowing it, and I going to pay it back each week, bit by bit. But just as I was taking the money, she walked into the room. I panicked. I only meant to push her out of the way, but she ended up falling badly and was left with bruising and broken bones, and was in hospital for weeks. So I've been done for assault and robbery, and didn't get bail. I never meant to hurt her. I know taking the money was wrong, but I only meant to borrow it. I had no intention of injuring her. It was like a reflex action when I pushed her, more like an accident. Yet, here I am; locked up at my age.'

I felt bad for the old lady in hospital, but I couldn't help but feel for Dotty. In her own way, and in her own mind, she was trying to do right by her family. Sadly, she hadn't even thought about the potential consequences of her misguided sense of help. And how could she have? Poor Dotty, I thought.

Adjusting to each other's ways and habits was a bit of a challenge at first for the both of us. One morning, Dotty woke up and had the shock of her life.

'What the bloomin' heck are you doing?' she shouted. She shrieked even louder when I didn't answer, and when she realised she wasn't getting anywhere she finally shut up.

When I finished, I picked my prayer mat up off the floor and came over to her.

'I was praying, Dotty.' I realised my kneeling, bending, and prostrating had caused her to freak out.

'Praying?' She sounded genuinely horrified.

'Yes, I was praying on my prayer mat, and when we, that's us Muslims, when we pray, we have to ignore everything around us and really try and connect with God for those few minutes, unless, of course, there's an emergency.'

'Well, I could have been shouting because of an emergency.'

'Not really. That's as bad as what I did when I was about four years old.'

'Why? What happened?'

'I'd been left at home with my grandma. No one else was in. My mum and dad had to go out. My dad keyed in his mobile number into the house phone and showed me how to redial, and said I could call him and mum, but only if there was an emergency. So I called them. Naturally, they were very worried and asked me what the emergency was. I told them I couldn't watch my favourite cartoon, as neither my grandma nor I knew how to switch on the new television. My dad said that wasn't an emergency, but to a four-year old it really was.' We both laughed.

'So, what's all this praying malarkey then?'

'It's just that. We are supposed to pray five times a day, facing in the direction of Mecca. I didn't use to pray all that much before, in fact hardly ever, but since I've been in here, I've got an awful lot of time on my hands. And to be honest, it helps. Truly, God's just about all I've got now. And suddenly, I've become really good with the old *namaz*. That's the Urdu word for prayer.'

'What's Urdu?' she asked, and we laughed again.

Before long, we started getting along like a house on fire. I think Dotty was a godsend for me, and she enjoyed having me to talk to as well. Suddenly the days weren't so boring anymore. Dotty had a wicked sense of humour, which helped me to banish the negative thoughts to the back of my mind. I started teaching her Urdu for fun, and she even learnt some swear words from me. She said she was going to use them on her neighbour Eileen, and she said that next time Eileen annoyed her, she was going to call her a *kuthi*!

'The fact that she won't know it means "bitch" will be all the more fun!' Dotty said, with a mischievous laugh to boot.

We both enrolled in some courses to help us pass the time, and learnt some valuable skills along the way. Although I had to admit that Dotty's attempt to stitch textiles to produce a fashionable garment was probably one of the funniest things I had ever seen. The idea was to make a simple blouse. There were to be no buttons or zips. It would be nice and easy. But she managed to sew the front of the blouse upside down, and inside out, and it had been cut about a foot shorter than the back.

By her own admission, Dotty became a sort of stand-in mum for me, and each day we laughed. On some days, we cried together. I missed my mum, and she missed her daughter, so we were the perfect temporary fix for each other.

Chapter 32: The Phone Call

IT WAS THE DAY BEFORE the start of my trial. I was in the prison gym with Dotty for our allotted session, and we were having a rowing competition. The beads of sweat trickled down my face, as I was pulling away with full force. Along with praying, the gym had become an obsession that helped me get through the day. I was getting fitter and faster on the treadmill and cross trainer, and was pumping weights like a semi-pro. Dotty pretended she was working hard on the rowing machine, but I knew her well enough by now to be able to spot her cheating methods. She would do anything to wriggle out of working hard; that was Dotty. We were in the middle of arguing, as we had stopped, so I could tell her she wasn't trying properly, which of course she denied, when a Prison Officer came out of the blue to tell me my brief was on the phone.

'Hello.' I said, as I grabbed the telephone in excitement. The buzz you got from knowing that someone from the outside world had called you was something else.

'Hi Selina, it's me, Mo.'

'Hi Mo, I figured it was you. How are you? What's up?' I was intrigued as I didn't usually get unexpected calls.

'I'm absolutely fine. I just thought I would phone and check on you, to ask how you are.'

'That's really good of you Mo, but you don't normally do that. You usually come in when you need to discuss things, otherwise I don't hear from you. Is there something wrong?'

'No, no, not at all. Nothing's wrong. It's just that...' he hesitated.

'It's just what? Come on Mo, you're scaring me here.'

'You know yourself, your case isn't looking great, and we are pretty much clutching at straws. Things aren't good. I don't want to say too much at this stage. I don't really know how it's going to pan out and affect everything, but there has been a development in your case.'

'A development? What kind of a development?'

'I don't want to say until I'm sure about what's going on.'

'But I don't understand.'

'Oh, before I forget to mention it, I saw your mum this morning. She came in just to get an update on things, and she told me to tell you that Henna is expecting.'

'What? Again? So soon!'

'Yes, that's what she said.'

'Oh my Lord, I bet she's barely coping with the baby as it is. He's just gone six months. I think it's safe to assume that it was a—happy—accident.'

'Selina, just hold the line will you?' He put me on hold for a half a minute or so, which only served to increase my sense of agitation as to what this call was all about. I still felt totally in the dark.

'I'm sorry Selina,' he said when he returned to me. 'I've got a really important call holding; I'm going to have to go. I will talk to you soon. Take care.'

'But Mo—.' The phone line clicked, and went dead. It was no use. He was gone.

I tossed and turned that night, unable to rest or sleep, and even Dotty noticed, as she banged on my bed from underneath to tell me to stop fidgeting. Every time I flipped and turned, my top bunk creaked, and Dotty kept telling me to be quiet. In the end, she had almost as bad a night's sleep as me.

'I wonder what he meant,' I said to Dotty in the morning, trying hard to get the words out amidst a yawn. 'What if it's bad news?'

I had woken up super early, and was finishing my makeup in readiness for my appearance in court, as today was the first day of my trial.

'He would have told you, or better still, he would have visited,' Dotty tried to reassure me, and then yawned too. 'I'm sure you're worrying about nothing. You know what these solicitors are like. He probably just made the call so he could claim for it on his bill. I bet he's got a flash car hasn't he? How do you think he pays for that?'

'Not Mo,' I retaliated, surprising myself as to how defensive I was about him. 'I mean, he does have a sporty BMW, but he's not like that. He actually cares. He's a good guy.'

'And good-looking, too, from what you've said. Do they even exist? Good-looking good guys,' laughed Dotty. 'Cos if you come across any more, chuck a spare one my way will you? They can even be good looking bad boys—I'd love to grow old disgracefully!' She laughed with wild abandonment.

'Dotty!' I said it with a disapproving look, yet I was unable to disguise my half smile.

There was quite a lot of traffic congestion on the way to the court, and the prison van arrived with only minutes to spare before the scheduled start time of ten o'clock. Perhaps it was better this way, as it saved me from sitting and waiting anxiously in yet another cell.

So this was it. This jury was now going to decide whether they believed I acted in self-defence, or whether I murdered Zubair in cold blood.

Chapter 33: The Trial

WHEN I WAS BROUGHT UP to the dock, I turned around and looked toward the public gallery. I could see mum and Adam. Henna wasn't there. I assumed she didn't come because she wasn't feeling well as a result of her pregnancy. My mum smiled at me, but the smile didn't hide the fear that was clearly visible in her eyes. She was scared of what was going to become of her child, frightened of what the court would decide. Many people from our local community had turned up in support of Sajda and her sons, as they still believed Zubair had been an upstanding man of impeccable morals. At last, I spotted Sajda. She looked at me with an air of cold, indignant defiance, sending a spiky chill right through me. I quickly turned around to face the front toward the wigged and robed judge. I could see Mo sitting next to my barrister, and he gave me a reassuring little nod of the head. I waited nervously for the proceedings to begin.

The first two days consisted of opening statements from both barristers, and the testimonies from the prosecution witnesses—the police officers and forensics experts. It had been difficult to listen to, hearing in very technical detail about the way I had killed him; from which angle, how deep the scissors had gone, and how quickly he had died.

On the third day of the trial, the Prosecution finished off their case by calling Sajda to the stand.

Sajda's testimony was clear, concise and damning. When she was asked about the relationship between her husband and myself, she didn't hold back.

'My husband had been helping Selina with her Economics work out of the goodness of his heart. However, he told me that he was left with no choice but to cancel the remaining study sessions because this girl had developed quite a crush on him. It was most inappropriate. She even asked him to come up to her bedroom on her wedding day. Her mother had always treated my husband as her younger brother, and consequently he had always behaved like an uncle towards her. But she was infatuated with him. From what my husband had told me, and from what I had seen, I would say she was obsessed. It was embarrassing.'

My heart sank, and in my mind, I resigned myself to the fact that Sajda had just thrown any hopes I may have harboured of not going to prison for a very long time straight off the edge of a cliff. In that moment, I felt utter despair, such despair as I had never experienced before.

The following morning, it was the defence team's turn to lay out their case and call their witnesses to the stand, or rather, call their only witness—me. I figured this was going to be one of, if not *the* most difficult thing that I would ever have to do. My palms were sweating, and my head thumped in sync with my heartbeat. I was going through it all in my head, psyching myself up to take the stand, when my barrister, David Evans, took to his feet.

'Your Honour,' he began, addressing the judge, 'some new evidence has come to light, and whilst I appreciate that this is at a very late stage in the proceedings, I would respectfully ask for a private conference in your chambers with yourself and the prosecution barrister with regard to this.'

'I object your Honour,' declared the prosecution barrister, briskly jumping to his feet. 'It is clearly contrary to court rules and protocol to allow any evidence to be produced so late in the day, mid-trial.'

'Yes, but ultimately, it is up to your Honour to exercise your discretion if you so wish,' replied my barrister.

'Hmmm,' mumbled the judge, in a disgruntled manner. 'Really, this is quite irregular, Mr Evans.'

'Yes, your Honour, I accept that, and I can only apologize for any inconvenience, but the significance of the new evidence is such that I feel it would be against the interests of justice for the court to dismiss it without at least hearing some details pertaining to it, especially given the grave indictment of murder against my client.'

'Very well then,' replied the judge, with a sigh, 'to my chambers now, both of you.'

I was left to wonder what on earth was going on. What new evidence? And why hadn't I been told? I was completely stumped.

After a short adjournment, we were all called back into the courtroom.

My barrister sprung up onto his feet once again.

'The defence would now like to call its first witness, Shabana Sultan,' said my barrister.

Shabana! Haji Sultan's granddaughter? I was flabbergasted.

After the swearing in and confirmation of her name and address, my barrister asked Shabana how she had known Zubair.

'He was a very good friend of the family. Everybody in the community knew him, really.'

'Can you tell me what happened Shabana?'

'Yes. It was a few years ago, when I was fourteen. My dad's car was off the road, and Zubair offered to give me a lift to school as it was en-route for him on his way to work. Like I said, the families knew each other very well. Everyone thought Zubair was this great man, and completely trusted him. He was to give me a lift for four or five days, just in the mornings as there was no one else available at that time. The school was quite a distance away, so it was a real help to my dad when he offered. Anyway, the first couple of days were fine, nothing odd to report. He asked me about my studies, my subjects, that kind of thing; and I answered politely. Then on the third day…' Shabana paused.

'What happened on the third day?'

Shabana hesitated for a few moments longer. She became teary, and took out a tissue from her pocket. She looked down for a few seconds, then lifted her head and continued.

'On the third day he didn't drive straight to the school. He took a turn before we got to the school, and drove on for a good few minutes. He claimed he had to get petrol and he wouldn't take long, and I wouldn't be late for school. But then he took another turn down a quiet little lane, and once he had driven the car to a remote spot, he….sexually assaulted me.'

I felt her agony, as she stood there; her face looking pained, as though she was reliving it all somewhere in the back of her mind, a place that nobody else could see.

'Did you tell your family what he did?'

'No.'

'Why not?'

'Because he threatened me that if I spoke to anyone about it, he would tell my family about my secret boyfriend. He had obviously hung around for a while one morning after dropping me off, and saw me with a boy. I was scared stiff.'

'What happened the next day?'

'Nothing, because I didn't go to school for the rest of the week; I told my parents that I felt ill. And my dad got the car sorted after that.'

'Did you tell anyone at all?'

'Yes, I confided in my best friend at school, but I swore her to secrecy.'

My barrister then referred to the witness statement of Shabana's friend confirming this, which the judge read through.

The prosecution's cross-examination was gruelling. As Shabana and her friend knew me from school, albeit they were a couple of years my junior, and our families were well acquainted, the Prosecution implied that Shabana and her friend had concocted this story to try and help my case. Shabana tried her best to deal with the ruthless questioning, however, she got herself tangled up quite a few times, when she was placed under intense scrutiny, and her every word was dissected in minutiae detail.

'So, I put it to you, that you have come here today with some sense of misguided loyalty towards your friend,' said the prosecutor.

'No, that's not true,' Shabana responded.

'Is it not? Are you saying you would not help her if she were in trouble?'

'No, I mean, yes—'

'Which one is it? You would, or you wouldn't?' he asked.

'I would help her.'

'And you think she needs your help today, do you?'

'Maybe, I'm not sure. Yes, I think she does.'

'Therefore, you must think she has a very weak case without your testimony. And I put it to you, that in your quest to help Selina, you would go so far as to lie for her!'

I had no doubt that Shabana was telling the truth, but I wasn't sure that her performance in the witness stand had done me any good, and perhaps it may even have damaged my case if the jury believed the assertions made about her fabricating the story.

My head just dropped towards the floor, and I tried bravely to fight back the tears.

'The Defence would like to call its next witness, Raheela Akbar,' announced my barrister.

Raheela? Who was Raheela? I racked my brains, but then remembered that in fact, I did know someone by that name. The only Raheela I knew of was Sajda's sister. Zubair's sister-in-law. I didn't know her very well. She got married and moved away years ago. I only saw her once in a blue moon, at weddings and stuff like that. Why was she here? What did she have to do with anything? She didn't know anything about me and Zubair. She wasn't even around at the time that the rape or his death occurred.

Raheela was dressed in a long, dark grey skirt, black ankle boots, and a fitted black blazer. She wore a nude pink and light grey coloured headscarf, which was secured to the front of her blazer with a sparkly, butterfly shaped brooch. She took to the witness stand, and held the Quran in her right hand.

'I swear by Almighty Allah, that the evidence that I shall give shall be the truth, the whole truth and nothing but the truth.'

She confirmed her name and address to the court.

'Can you tell us your relationship with the deceased, Zubair Qureshi?' asked my barrister.

'Yes. I am his wife's sister.' She looked towards Sajda in the public gallery briefly, then turned her attention back toward the questioning.

'And how old were you when they married?'

'I was fourteen.'

'And what were your first impressions of Zubair Qureshi?

'Well, at first I thought he was a wonderful brother-in-law. He was refreshing to be around; he was great company, intelligent, witty, talkative. I could see my sister was besotted with him and could understand why; he was handsome, attentive, and had a great sense of humour.

'And the rest of your family, how did they feel?'

'They really liked him. We all felt totally at ease with him.'

'I understand you used to babysit for your sister?'

'Yes, about a year after the marriage, the first baby came along, and a year later, Sajda decided to go back to work for a couple of evenings a week. It was agreed that I would babysit. It would only be for about an hour as then Zubair would be back from work.'

'Did anything happen when you went over to babysit?'

Raheela's face turned pale, and she asked for a glass of water.

'Not to worry, please, take your time,' my barrister said to her, reassuringly.

'Well, that's when it started, when I was babysitting.'

'That's when *what* started?'

Raheela cleared her throat before she continued.

'That's when the abuse started. Sexual abuse. And the rapes.'

There were audible gasps from the public gallery, after which whispers and murmurs began to get louder. Many from the local community had turned up in support of Sajda and her sons, and in support of a man they had firmly believed to have been a descent, respectable human being. These same people were now ruminating and whispering amongst themselves.

I turned and looked back, and I could see that my mum was sitting on the edge of her seat whilst she heard these revelations. Sajda was visibly shocked; she looked aghast. She appeared as white as a sheet, and had one hand over her open mouth. Her sons, who were sat either side of her, were trying their best to console her. People in the public gallery continued to talk as they tried to digest the disturbing exposé that was unfolding before them.

'Silence in the courtroom!' shouted the judge. 'No talking in court. That is an order. Anyone in defiance of this order will be held in contempt of court. Mr Evans, please continue with your witness.'

'How old were you at the time?'

'I was only sixteen years old when it first occurred.'

'And how often were you abused or raped?'

'On many occasions, too many to give you a precise number, but really it was whenever the opportunity presented itself.'

'Did you tell anyone about this at the time?'

'No.'

'Why not?'

'I was so young, and I was very scared of him. I was petrified of telling anyone, as he convinced me that if I said anything he would make sure I came out looking like a tart who had come on to him. The emotional blackmail was unbearable for me. He was the apple of everyone's eye. My sister was totally mad for the guy; and my parents thought they had found the perfect son-in-law. He had me under his cast-iron fist, and I couldn't see a way out. I just tried my best to avoid being alone with him as much as I could.'

Poor Raheela, I thought. How awful.

'What happened after you finished school?'

'University was how I managed to get away from him. I was offered a place at Leicester, and convinced my parents to let me go study away from home. They were reluctant at first back in those days, being a bit old-fashioned about letting the daughters go away from home to study. But I managed to talk them round as there was another girl from my school who had also got a place at Leicester University, and our families knew each other quite well. So it was agreed that us two girls would share digs, and this made my parents feel better about it. I then met my husband whilst I was down there, and so straight after my degree I got married and ended up staying there.'

'Why did you never tell anyone about the abuse?'

'I didn't really see the need once I had moved away. As far as I was concerned I was free of him and didn't need to think about all that ever again.

'Did you tell your husband?'

'No. Well, not until very recently'

'Why not?'

'Because, I knew that I would still have to see Zubair occasionally at family events, and it was better for me to keep my own counsel. It would prevent any awkwardness. Also, I just didn't want to remember any of it. I wanted to shut it away and never be reminded of it again.'

'So, why have you come forward now?'

'When I heard about Selina's case, it all came flooding back to me. I felt depressed and couldn't bear the thought that she might end up in prison when that scumbag had it coming to him anyway. I regretted not saying anything at the time. If I had, then maybe he wouldn't have been in a position to attack Selina, and she wouldn't be locked up. I have kids of my own, and neither they nor my husband, in fact, nobody at all, knew about what I had suffered. I did question whether I should open up this can of worms. But after a lot of deliberating and soul searching, I thought that to act upon what I knew was the only thing to do. I summoned the courage to talk to my husband. He was very supportive about it all, and he encouraged me to come forward. I realised the consequences of doing so, not least the ramifications with my sister and wider family, but it was the right thing to do.'

My eyes welled up once again, both in disbelief, but also with a sad sense of familiarity with what I had just heard. I thought about how difficult it must have been for this woman to drag all this up from the past. I of all people knew how she must have felt at the prospect of having to relive the traumas she would sooner forget, but in a way it was worse for her, for she had to delve into painful memories from such a long time ago, ones she probably thought were dead and buried, and that too with the inevitable fall-out from her family. I wished I had been brave straight after the rape.

The Prosecution barrister's cross-examination of Raheela was even fiercer than that he had inflicted upon Shabana. He tried his utmost to discredit her testimony, claiming that there was no evidence of what Raheela was alleging, and he questioned her motives for not speaking at the time, and doing so now after all these years. However, unlike Shabana, whose youth and naivety had let her down, Raheela displayed a steely grit, and a degree of maturity, which meant that despite his best efforts, the Prosecutor was unable to significantly damage

Raheela's testimony, as she came across as a very honest, strong and credible witness.

The judge then spoke for the first time in a while, addressing both the barristers, briefly, but crisply.

'Gentlemen, my chambers, now.'

The proceedings were adjourned as the judge disappeared through his door that was situated behind him, and the barristers made their way to see him.

Over an hour had passed, as I sat in the cell below the court, wondering about my fate, wondering what the legal eagles were all saying to each other. They were, no doubt, speaking in fancy rhetoric and drawn-out phrases, but I just wanted to know in the simplest language possible what was going to happen to me.

The court re-summoned, and this time the prosecution barrister stood up.

'Your honour, in light of the evidence that has been presented to the court today, and after considering all legal aspects of this case, I can confirm to the court that the Crown Prosecution Service no longer believes that it would be in the public interest to continue with the prosecution against Selina Hussain, therefore all charges against her are dropped forthwith.'

The Judge looked at me, took off his glasses, and without hesitation, he uttered five magical words. 'You are free to go.'

As soon as I heard those words, I fell to the floor in a big messy heap, just as I had done in my bedroom back on the 14th of June last year. Only this time, my emotions were strikingly different. I cried softly, and quietly. But I cried my heart out. I hadn't dared to even dream about walking out of prison. I didn't let myself think about ever seeing the outside world again. I was sure I would be locked up for a long, long time. And to be told this, I was delirious.

I looked up and saw the relief in my mother's face, and turned and caught the glimpse of sheer elation in Mo's smile when he rushed over and helped me back onto my feet. He was followed very shortly by my mum, and the witnesses who had turned up today to give evidence. We all embraced, and cried, and cheered, in a huddle of emotional union and solidarity.

But amidst the triumphant and joyous celebrations, my thoughts turned to Dotty, and a pang of sadness crept into me. She was going to be all alone in that prison cell now. My heart sank at the thought. I knew she would feel the fear, the fear you only experience in a place like prison; the fear of loneliness, the fear of abundant isolation, the fear of thinking so much you think your head will burst, the fear that you might go mad if you are cooped up a second longer. Sometimes you were convinced that you were dreaming and tried to wake yourself up, but then you realised that, in fact, it was reality. Other times you would have a nightmare, but wish it was real, so you didn't have to spend another moment in your cell, because anything was better than that. I was so grateful to Dotty, to this woman who had made my life in that dump bearable, and even enjoyable at times. I was going to miss her from the bottom of my heart.

As I stepped gingerly out of the court building with Mo and my family at my side, I stopped and took a long deep breath. I looked up at the sky; there were a few bands of dusky blue hues peeping through, but mostly it was beginning to cloud over and was predominantly greyish. It was grey, and it was beautiful. I scanned around me and took in the colours of the trees. I looked down at the dark solid tarmac I was stood on, and then stared at all the different cars in the car park. I closed my eyes gently. I listened to the sound coming from the traffic up ahead, and the hum of an aeroplane above me in the sky. I could hear a crow squawking, and thought I heard the familiar sound of magpie. It was all music to my ears; the greatest compositions of Tchaikovsky and Beethoven were not a patch on the melodious sounds of the outside world that were filtering into my ears right now.

'Come on, I thought you wanted to get out of this place,' said Mo.

I opened my eyes and took a long, deep breath. 'Yes. I'm ready.'

Chapter 34: The reunion

THE DAY AFTER MY RELEASE, mum decided to cook a big meal to celebrate. The sheer joy I felt at being back home with my mum and brother again was inexplicable. To top it all off, Henna, together with her bump, Faisal, and my beautiful nephew had come over to our house to join in the family celebration. Kamran was so adorable, I felt as if I was going to melt there and then as soon as I laid eyes on him. He had grown so much since I had last seen him; he had a fine tuft of hair, and was now all smiles and chuckles. There had been a mix of tears and jubilations from everyone in my family since my release.

Mum had made enough food to feed an army, but on this occasion I let rip, and I stuffed myself with the best home cooked *chapli* kebabs, *channa chaat*, chicken *pilau*, *achari* lamb and *tarka daal*, and *parathas*, and I swore that I would never ever take good food for granted again. I didn't have room for the sweet rose scented *lab-e-shireen*, or the reassuringly comforting *halwa* that my mum had also made. But I would find space in my tummy somehow for the desserts later; that was certain.

After all the food, weeping, joking and laughing, I sat down with a mug of hot tea in the living room. I noticed that my mum had changed the carpet. I didn't want to think about it today, but little things would always remind me. I just closed my eyes for a few seconds. I could hear the clatter of the dishes from the kitchen where mum and Henna were chattering away whilst they washed and cleared up. Faisal and Adam had popped out to go get some ice cream, and perhaps a cream cake or two, as Adam was never too keen on the Pakistani desserts. The baby was sound asleep. I breathed the scent of home deep into my lungs. I smelt a homey fragrance that exudes an underlying security you find nowhere else. I breathed in a calm serenity that only your home can give you. I inhaled the delicate scent of inner peace; if you search for it, you will surely find it here, I concluded. Home was not the place. I knew that now. Home was the people. My people. My family. I had missed them all so much.

After a good helping of pudding, and in my case, that meant a small portion each of them, the ones my mum had made and a slice of the Victoria sponge cake with a dollop of real dairy vanilla ice cream, we all sat together and I relaxed to the max, laying my head right back.

'Selina, there is something that you should know,' said mum, slightly apprehensively.

'What is it?' I asked, sitting up a little.

'It's Sohail.'

I sat up fully. 'What about him?'

'He's on his way up here. He wants to talk to you. He should be here soon. He only told me he was coming about an hour ago, and he phoned after he had set off. I'm sorry; he was really insistent and gave me no choice in the matter.'

I was not expecting this at all, and didn't know what to make of it.

'I just thought I would mention to you all,' Henna said, as she came and sat next to me, 'that there's something Faisal and I need to discuss with you all. We can all sit down and have a chat after Sohail leaves.'

* * *

Sohail greeted my mum at the door and then walked into the living room. He said his *salams* to everyone else. He looked as well turned out as ever; his hair was gelled back off his forehead, and he was wearing pale blue, designer jeans with a smart navy blue polo shirt. Once the initial niceties were over with, everyone else scarpered. Alone again, I thought to myself. I didn't envisage this the day after my return home.

'It's good to see you. You're looking well,' Sohail said to me as he sat on the other side of the three-seater sofa.

'Thanks,' I replied, ignoring the fact that he couldn't possibly have believed that I looked "well" as I looked gaunt and tired after my stint behind bars. My skin was pale, my hair was limp and my eyes had dark circles around them. Oh well.

'How are your parents? And your sister?' I asked out of politeness.

'They're all well. Everyone is fine. They were asking after you.' I didn't believe that either. If that had been the case, they would have come up with him, although I still didn't know why he had come up at all.

'You must be wondering what I'm doing here.'

'Well, yes, I was thinking that, to be honest.'

Sohail leaned over slightly and then shifted his body around so he could face me properly. I sat still and waited to hear what he had to say.

'When you came back up here, things between us were left on such a disagreeable note. It hasn't sat right with me ever since. Selina, I'm not proud of the way I treated you. When I heard about—about what had happened to you, I felt really terrible. You should have told me.'

'You didn't want to know. In any event, would it have made any difference? Be honest. Anyway, you were the one who wanted to end it all, as I recall. You made that decision.'

'And now I regret it. I've had a lot of time to think about it all. If I had known, then perhaps—'

'I gave you the opportunity, but you weren't interested. You had just shut yourself off, completely. It was as though nothing I said or could have said would have mattered. You were seeing red. You couldn't stand the sight of me.'

'But that was then. I'm here now. Surely that counts for something,' he said quite forcefully, with his palms upturned.

'Selina, please, can you find it in your heart to forget everything that happened in the past, and maybe start again. I still care for you. In fact, I still love you. I have always loved you, and I can't imagine loving any other woman as I do you. I haven't been able to get you out of my head.'

Sohail spoke with a sharp tinge of passion in his voice, albeit his words ended tenderly, and his hands trembled ever so slightly as he placed them into mine. His touch felt warm, and reassuringly familiar, and his hands covered mine like a cosy pair of gloves that fit just right. My heart fluttered as his thumb gently caressed my palm in a soothing, circular motion.

'That time we spent together before you left was the happiest of my life. And I want it back. You are still my wife. It is my duty to protect you, I know that, and I also acknowledge that it is a duty I failed in miserably when we were together. I realise now that my love for you is strong enough for me to never make that mistake again. We could try and make it work. I'm willing to try if you are. Sure, I was angry at the time, but I didn't know the full picture. I feel differently now. I want you back. And my family is fine with it as well. They know it's my decision. And I will never, ever let you down again. I promise to stand by you, no matter what, to protect you and keep you from harm's way so far as it's in my power to do so. So, what do you say?'

Chapter 35: A declaration of love

AS SOHAIL SPOKE, I looked down at the new carpet. I was so glad that mum had changed the carpet. This one was patterned; it was a sort of pale, charcoal blue, with little green paisley designs on it. The last one was a plain, muddy, coffee shade. Colour is good, I thought. I preferred the new one. I liked the change.

I looked back up toward him and knew that I saw the same Sohail as I had married. He looked the same, pretty much sounded the same, and probably still thought in the same way, despite his words to the contrary. But I wasn't the same. I definitely wasn't that person anymore.

'Sohail, it's really good of you to come all this way to speak to me like this. But the thing is that—it's too late. Sometimes when a moment is lost, it's lost forever. Our moment was when I got back from the hospital and we sat down to talk. I needed you to take that moment, to grasp it, and be there for me, for us, but you didn't. And now it's gone. So I'm sorry, but I can't go back. *We* can't go back. After everything that's happened, I need to move forward. And I can't do that as things stand. So, I would be grateful if you would agree to a...divorce.'

Sohail's body stiffened. Not much more was said after that. He left in a state of shock. A part of me felt some sympathy for him, but the rest of me felt the urge to forge ahead like some warrior princess. He was my past. I wanted to look to the future, my future.

* * *

I walked into the coffee shop where I'd agreed to meet. It was a rainy, blustery day, and I had been virtually blown through the door by the would-be tempest that was howling outside.

I was a couple of minutes early, so I went to buy the coffees, and then in walked Mo. He seemed just as dishevelled as I had been when I had stumbled through the door, but that didn't detract from his stunning looks. His eyes still shone, and his face still glowed. The warmth of his smile suddenly lit up a grey, miserable day. Americano and skinny latte in hand, we found a table in the corner, one that was ideally tucked away for a good natter. In any event, the coffee house was quiet, as no doubt the weather was keeping people away.

'So, how have you been this past week? I haven't really heard much from you since the day you were released.' Mo spoke with what I felt was a little sigh in his words, although he didn't actually sigh.

'I'm sorry I haven't been in touch. There's been a lot going on. It's been really strange, just walking out and about, hanging the washing in the back yard, going to Mr Patel's corner shop for some milk and bread, catching the bus here today. It is all so surreal. I was only in prison for three months, and had it not been for those witnesses I could have been in there an awful lot longer, but just in those three months, I almost forgot about the normal, beautifully mundane stuff that life is made of. And I can't thank you enough Mo, for everything you have done for me, right from day one when you came to see me at the police station.'

Mo hesitated. He opened his mouth to speak, but then no words came out.

'Is something wrong Mo?' I asked him.

'Wrong? No, nothing's wrong, well, not yet anyway.'

'What do you mean, not yet? You're not making any sense.'

'I don't know, maybe I should just come out with it.'

'Come out with what?'

He took a deep breath and continued. 'You know how I feel about you, well, how I've always felt about you, it's never been a secret. I've always liked you. But when all that stuff happened, and you got locked up, it panicked me. And obviously, it wasn't in a way I would usually feel for a client. It was a stifling, all-consuming sort of a dread, a fear that you may be inside for a long time, and I wouldn't see you. And then I knew. I knew that I cared about you deeply. I knew that I, that I—loved you. My life just revolved around you for every waking moment. I couldn't think about anything apart from getting you out of there. And now that you're out, I still can't stop thinking about you. I think about you all the time, day and night. I want to know—I *need* to know—is there any chance of us ever being more than friends? Do you feel *anything* for me? Is there any possibility we might have some sort of a future together? I want to be with you. I've tried to fight it, but it's no use. I can't just be friends with you. I love you, Selina. I need more. I want more.'

I listened quietly and intently, and looked at his lovely face as he spoke. He had beautifully chiselled features, his eyes were the most enticing I had ever seen, and the way he looked at me made my heart flutter. I think I loved him too, in a way. I wasn't sure, but I must be pretty damn close to it, I thought to myself. He was also the most caring man I had ever known. But could I love him back as he did me? Was I ready to love him as completely as he was ready to love me? My thoughts and feeling were all tangled up, like a mixed-up ball of fluffy wool. I held his hand, closed my eyes for a couple of minutes to allow my thoughts to unravel. He waited patiently. My thoughts flowed begrudgingly at first. I tightened my grip on his strong, steady hand, and pushed myself to think harder. I opened my eyes, and saw his soft green eyes looking straight back into mine. And then I knew. I knew the answer.

Chapter 36: The final flight

MO'S ANTICIPATION GREW, as we sat in silence for a few seconds longer. He nervously stroked the nape of his neck with his free hand, and he waited for me to say something. I cupped both my hands securely around his hand that was still on the table.

'Mo, I can never ever repay you for everything you have done for me. No words can ever be enough, and nothing I could do for you could make up for it. I'm beyond flattered to hear you speak of me in this way. And if I am truly honest, with you and with myself, then I have to admit that I do love you, too.'

His face softened, as some of the tension it had been carrying dissipated, and he smiled a smile that would light a whole city.

'But—I can't be with you.'

'What? I don't understand, you said—'

'I know this may not make sense, but I'm going to try and explain myself anyway. You see, up until now, throughout this young life of mine, I have always been defined by men. For the most part, it was my father. My whole life revolved around him. He was the centre of the universe and whatever he said was gospel. His opinion was sacrosanct, and his advice was priceless. After he went, my life was empty without what I saw as his guiding light. And then came Zubair, he forced himself upon me in more ways than one. The whole course of my life changed because of the actions of this one man. So to escape this man, I ran to another, seeing Sohail as a solution to all my problems, instead of facing what had happened to me head on, and finding the courage to deal with it, however painful that might have been for me and my family. May be if I had done that in the first place, then, well, who knows, eh? The point I'm trying to make is that the direction of my life so far has been determined because of the men in it. The thing is, we have decided to move to Manchester, all three of us. Henna has asked us to move closer to them. And I think my mum really wants to be nearer to my sister now that she is expecting her second baby. To be honest, she could do with the help. Also, it will be a fresh start for all of us, and particularly for me, as staying here will always remind me of the most painful moments of my life. I'm hoping to finally start university, and as you know, there's no shortage of universities in Manchester. If I stay, then it will be the same thing all over again. I will be choosing the course of my future because of yet another man, and even though I think I do love you Mo, I can't do that. I need to do what's right for me. I'm not leaving just for my family, but for myself. If I stay, it will be for the wrong reasons, and whilst I can't think of any better reason to remain here than you, I know that doing that would not be the right decision. Who knows about tomorrow, but today, right now, I can't give you the answer you want.'

Mo, teary-eyed and desolate, continued to gaze at me, but he knew from the determined look in my eyes that my mind was made up. We parted with a heart-rending goodbye, and as I walked away from him, I did so with a heavy feeling of regret, as I thought about what might have been. Had I just walked away from the best thing that might ever have happened to me?

* * *

Before getting into the car, I gave one last lingering look... at the street I had spent my whole life in, the home I had grown up in. I was leaving for the final time. Despite everything that had happened here, it was difficult to say goodbye to this little place that had been my world, my whole existence. I knew every little patch of this street, where I had played hopscotch, and pedalled up and down on my bike. The tears burnt in my eyes as the cold wind hit my face, and swept through my long hair. My heart was so heavy with an aching feeling of nostalgia; I had never before felt such a longing for the past as I did at that moment. I was leaving behind the physical memories of my father, and the precious memories of my childhood. But I couldn't stay. Staying was not an option. It would only ever remind me of all the agony of recent years.

Disappointing Mo had been one of the most difficult things I had ever done, and I had felt a wave of regret reverberate through me the minute I had walked away from him. Had I really done the right thing? Just because I had suffered at the hands of other men, and they had treated and judged me unjustly, it did not mean Mo would do the same. But deep down, I knew I didn't really fear unfairness or mistreatment at the hands of Mo. I had grown to love him. He was kind, generous and warm; a gem amongst men. But at this point in my life, there had to be more, I had to look at the bigger picture. I needed to take a step away from the confusing trail of mess that had penetrated my life over the last few years, and that meant stepping away from Mo, too.

Albeit with a heavy heart, I knew I had to leave, and carve my own path in life, in my own way, without the need to please or fear or appease any man. I had to do it because it was what I wanted, not because it was forced upon me, or demanded of me, or expected of me. I had to do this for me, and for me alone.

The time had now arrived for the kite to fly away—and not look back. It was time to fly away for good.

More books from
Harvard Square Editions: